THE SWINE

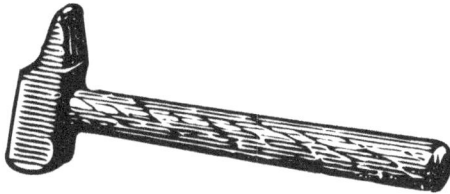

SIMON MCHARDY & SEAN HAWKER

Cover artwork by **warlocklord**
Cover design by **Drew Stepek** of Booksaw & godless.com

First Printing: October 2022
Potter's Grove Press, LLC
www.pottersgrovepress.com

ISBN: 978-1-951840-62-4

Dedicated to all those who kindly lent their names, but not their characters, to this story: Janie C., Matt Clarke, Marian Echevarria, Donna A Latham, Corrina (with two Rs) Morse, Renée Nieuwenhuis, Doll Peule and John Tomlinson.

This book is also dedicated to Samantha Hawkins and Tara Losacano for their tireless support of indie horror.

CHAPTERS

Sledgehammer 1

Cereal Pansy 12

Little Jonokuchi 21

Spastic Cock 28

Inbred Weirdo 36

Twirling Ballerinas 47

Titheads 55

Minced Legs 64

The Jousting Pig Dwarf 73

Klo Daax Ag Bodar Toz 81

Pancakes 89

Food For Ol' Sogash 96

Hog Roast 102

Szat 108

Going To Valhalla 116

Sumo Superstar 123

SLEDGEHAMMER

The window slid up and shut out the ominous wall of looming trees. Their long, sinewy branches stretched out like the arthritic fingers of an old crone eager to grab her and pull her deep into the forest. Corrina loathed being this far away from the city. The surrounding countryside unnerved her. The sulfuric stench of bog peat soil and the sour dampness of the rainforest caught in her throat and made her want to retch.

Savage River National Park, Tasmania was a primeval wilderness, an untamed region of isolated buttongrass moorlands and river gorges flanked by steep mountain ranges. Corrina shuddered. Here, nature was a malevolent entity out to scare, hurt and consume her. She much preferred the safety and comfort of lavish, five-star hotels. Thoughts of basking in the hot sun on a white, sandy beach, sipping a large, exotic cocktail teased her. The car sped on along the dirt road, rocking unsteadily over the uneven ground. Barry, her husband, had a lead foot. His attention flitted between switching radio stations and the few feet of visible road ahead of him, illumined by the car's headlamps.

The sibilant white noise of channel hopping pissed Corrina off, but she dug her fingers into her thighs and fought to hold her tongue. Any criticism of Barry's driving, especially after several hours of being on the road, would undoubtedly provoke a blistering tirade of abuse and escalate into an angry quarrel. She was tired and short-tempered. Her large, distended belly ached from the thuds of her baby's incessant kicks. Corrina swallowed and kept her voice light. "How many more miles is it until we get to the campsite? It's already pretty dark." She knew he was lost but wanted to hear him acknowledge it.

"Not much longer," Barry replied, his eyes fixed on the radio. "We should get there by seven, seven-thirty at the latest." Barry fancied himself as a rugged, macho outdoorsman even though he worked selling mobility scooter insurance over the phone and rarely ventured into the countryside. He binge-watched television programs where people lived semi-naked in the dusty outback and used bushcraft skills to survive. He would provide Corrina with a running commentary on how he was a real expert on starting fires, erecting shelters, and catching food with improvised snare traps. It was all a load of hot air, and Corrina knew it. On some days she couldn't believe she had let this man cum inside her and fertilise her eggs, but on other days, she couldn't bear to be apart from him.

A camping holiday in her condition wasn't the slightest bit appealing, but she knew that once the baby arrived, they'd have little to no opportunity to spend any quality time together. She'd choked back her fears and reluctantly agreed to a weekend in the wilderness. "I hadn't expected the sun to go down for at least a couple more hours. There aren't even any streetlights. No signposts either," Barry said. Corrina rolled her eyes and sighed. That was Barry's way of admitting he was lost. Barry glanced across at his wife, smiled, and patted her bare leg reassuringly. His white teeth gleamed in the car's dimly lit interior. "Mummy rang last night when you were taking a bath."

Corrina bit her bottom lip and clenched her fists until the skin went taut. She would rather spend a camping holiday stuck in a sleeping bag filled with live rats than be around that interfering, opinionated old bitch. "How is she?" Corrina was careful with her tone. Barry, for some unknown reason, was always on the defensive whenever they discussed his mother. The woman sparked off the couple's fiercest arguments. Nothing Corrina did was ever right, and now her mother-in-law was telling them how to raise her first grandchild. The baby should suckle from the breast until five years of age, just as Barry had.

"Oh, Mummy's fine except for the usual stuff. Spent an hour listening to her regale me with an up-to-date account of how the neighbour's Jack Russell had been pissing on the lawn and soiling her geraniums. She's bought a crossbow off eBay ready for the next time, and she said that her incontinence had been worse than ever."

Corrina puffed out a spurt of air. There was no escaping Mummy's frail bowels. "Sounds like an exciting phone call. Did you remind her to drop round and water my plants?"

"Yeah, she said she would." Barry squirmed in his seat and stared straight ahead. "She mentioned something else too."

"Let me guess. She's been complaining about me. She thinks I don't look after you well enough. She thinks I should be the dutiful wife and do all your laundry, cook all your meals, and massage your damn feet after a hard day at work." Corrina rubbed her temples. A tension headache threaded its way through her skull.

"Not at all. Mummy just said that maybe it would be best if she moved in with us when the baby arrives, so she can help with the child care."

"What the fuck, Baz? Are you fucking serious?" Corrina's face flushed in anger. She didn't want to argue, but Barry's mother was like petrol to a naked flame.

"Mummy's concerned you might get post-natal depression and neglect the baby's needs. She said because you're thirty-nine, there's a real possibility you don't have the same maternal instincts of a younger woman in her child-rearing prime. She means well."

"I know how old I am, thank you, Baz. We've had this conversation about her moving in with us more times than I care to remember. The answer is still, and will always be, no. I will never live in the same house as that witch." Spittle flew from Corrina's mouth and onto the dashboard. She pinched the bridge of her nose between thumb and forefinger and shook her head. Her headache escalated into a searing, scorching pain.

"And she's worried about being old and lonely now Daddy has passed, that's all. Her best friend had a heart attack and wasn't discovered until three weeks after she'd died. They found a dozen cats eating her body. One

4

apparently had been chewing on her face like it was biltong." Corrina furrowed her brow, folded her arms, and turned to stare out of the window. The wooden palisade of trees was still dense and suffocating to look at, but she smirked at the thought of her own mother-in-law being eaten as jerky by a horde of ravenous felines.

They drove on in silence. The thick mass of trees opened up only to be replaced by barren flatland that, in the darkness, looked like a sea of stagnant water. For the next mile, pale rays of moonlight broke through the billowing, black clouds to reveal the skeletal remains of abandoned buildings dotting the horizon. Rotted beams jutted out from collapsed roofs, piercing the leaden sky. "Mummy could have the spare room. We have plenty of space," Barry said finally.

"Screw your mother, Baz! It is not an option, and I am sick of her interfering in our lives. She needs to back off and let us raise this baby how we want."

"Okay, okay, calm down. I'm sorry I mentioned her."

"The old cow can't wait to wrap our baby around her finger, just as she has with you, Mummy's boy."

That pissed him off. Barry smacked his lips, and his eyes went steely cold. "I've got to stop and take a leak." He veered over to the edge of the road, unfastened his seat belt, and climbed out of the car without once looking at his wife. Barry paused, rolled his shoulders, and stretched his back. A chill wind whistled through the open door, drawing in the sharp stink of conifers, rot, and the brackish river.

"Shut the door. It's freezing in here," Corrina screeched. Barry slammed the door closed. She watched his silhouette disappear into the gloom and sucked in a few deep breaths while she fought for composure. "What a bloody cracking start to our camping holiday," Corrina muttered to herself as she sat alone in the car. She scanned the darkness outside and reached into her pocket. Her phone would be a welcome distraction from the eerie silence of the countryside. The signal was weak, but she could see there were no new messages from any of her girlfriends. Barry was taking his time. Unnerved, Corrina turned on the overhead light switch A comforting, dull, yellow glow washed over the interior, and she rubbed her hand over her belly. The baby had calmed down.

A groan echoed from outside. Corrina turned to see Barry stagger toward the car, clasping his stomach. His face was twisted in agony. The fool! She'd told him not to eat that damned, foot-long hot dog he'd bought at the gas station. The purplish, black-streaked sausage, dotted with syphilitic blisters, had wallowed in grease atop a filthy grill. But no, he hadn't listened and gobbled it down with lashings of ketchup from those little, red plastic pouches. Barry's body thumped into the side of the car, and he pressed his face against the window glass. His bloodshot eyes bulged from their sockets. "H-h-help me," he gurgled.

Corrina rolled her eyes and opened the window. "Serves you right for being greedy. I warned you about eating that dirty sausage." A large moon broke through the swirling clouds, and lustreless stars pricked through the tarry sky.

"Mummy, Mummy." Barry's lips trembled and then opened in a jaw-cracking, silent scream.

"Come on, Barry, cut out the dramatics. I'm weary. I'm cold, and your mother is never going to live with us." Barry's complexion turned eldritch white, a violent cough convulsed his body, and globs of blood spattered over the car's interior. Corrina half-rose from her seat and slumped back down in confusion. Barry's lips curled, and an anguished howl rumbled from deep within him. Corrina's chest tightened in terror at the inhuman sound.

"Oh my god, Baz." She heaved herself over to the driver's side, clambered from the car, and rushed to him. "What happened? Tell me! Did the gas station hot dog do this to you?" Blood and bile oozed from between his trembling fingers as he clutched at the slick strings of reddish flesh spilling from his gut. She pulled his hands toward her instinctively. There was a slosh, and warm fluid splashed against her exposed shins. Corrina peered down at the wet, steaming mound around her feet. A pile of shredded, glistening organs clung to her ankles and covered her shoes.

She screamed loudly enough for any nocturnal wildlife to flee for their lives. Panic-stricken, Barry reeled in the mud-coated flesh tubes dangling from the gaping cavity, hand over hand as if he were coiling up a rope. Sobbing, Corrina scooped up an armful of the slithery entrails and thrust them at the cavernous wound.

A sudden gust whipped the tree branches and showered them with twigs and leaves as they huddled by the car, feeding Barry's guts back into his mauled body. Corrina swallowed hard and hollered into the wind, "Oh god, Baz, we have to get you to a hospital. What fucking animal did this to you?"

She needn't have asked.

A huge, hulking shape rose up behind Barry. The towering figure wearing a pig-shaped mask and shouldering a sledgehammer strode toward them. A massive, dirt- and oil-encrusted hand clamped around Barry's head and squeezed. Barry's crimson eyeballs shot out of his head. Tethered by the optic nerves, they retracted and bounced against his pudgy cheeks. His head made a sickening crunch and exploded. Mushy, pink grey brain matter and broken teeth spewed over Corrina's face and chest. A cumshot of jelly hit her open mouth as his eyeballs popped. She scrambled backward, gagging on clumps of gore, and flung herself into the car. Her trembling fingers stabbed around the ignition button until they found their target.

The car didn't start. Barry had taken the key. Corrina cowered down in her seat and wailed in despair. Her husband lay by the side of the car next to his own expelled innards, his squashed head resembling a steamrollered possum. She scrabbled around in her pocket for her phone. The massive monstrosity thudded into the vehicle's flank and heaved the car up onto two wheels. Corrina's head cracked against the window. Her vision blurred and dark spots swam in front of her eyes.

She pressed a palm to the wound on her head and stared at the blood smearing her hand. More blood snaked through her eyebrows and pooled in her eyes before overflowing down her cheeks. The unborn baby kicked and churned. Corrina rubbed her distended belly desperate to comfort the little life inside her. Tears burst from her eyes and mingled with the blood. Images of Baz swirled before her. She had to save their baby. She had to run. The damaged door refused to budge, and she thumped down on the horn, hoping someone would hear it and come to her aid.

The pigman jumped onto the car. The roof dented and sagged under his titanic weight. The sledgehammer slammed down, smashed the windscreen, and showered Corrina in splinters of glass. She curled up into a ball and sobbed. The onslaught above her continued. Metalwork was torn apart, the concave roof dipped to meet her, and trapped her in the wreckage. The pigman thudded to the ground. A black, beady eye surrounded by leathery, coarse skin peered through the twisted metal and broken glass. Her bowels clenched. The cold, cruel eye stared at her. No trace of humanity flickered in the stony pupil.

She tried to scramble away, but thick, rough fingers coiled around her hair and jerked her out of her seat. Broken glass and shards of steel tore at her flesh as she was dragged through the mangled windscreen.

"Don't kill my baby, I'm begging you," she howled. "I don't want my baby to die. Please, let me go."

The pigman snorted and yanked her hair savagely in reply. Her head scraped through the narrow, jagged opening, grating off chunks of scalp and flesh, and revealing the ivory skull underneath. Corrina's torn and shredded face emerged from the crushed windscreen to confront a freakishly large porcine head framed by the bleak night sky.

Mist puffed from the beast's cracked, flared nostrils, and globules of grey snot dangled from the bristles above its lips. The nightmarish face above her wasn't a freakish mask worn by a human butcher but a man with the head of a pig. The pigman grasped her armpits, braced his foot by her head, and tugged. Corrina felt as if she were being dragged through a cheese grater. Curls of flesh peeled from her body. The pigman's muscled forearms strained as he forced her swollen belly through the windscreen.

"No! No, you're hurting my baby!" Her fingers clutched at the dashboard. The baby burst out from between her legs and squelched onto the seat. Rough hands yanked her from the car and tossed her onto the edge of the road beside her husband.

Griping cramps zigzagged through Corrina's gut, and her breath locked in her throat. Dark blood haemorrhaged from her crotch and puddled beneath her buttocks. The thin cry of a newborn wailed from the car like a police siren.

"Baz," she croaked, her voice barely above a whisper, "our baby." She reached out and grasped his hand. It was already cool to the touch. The pigman raised his snout to the moon, and a long, strident grunt broke from its throat as he smashed the sledgehammer into her mouth. Corrina's jaw wobbled uselessly as she tried to beg for the life of her baby.

The head of the hammer crunched into her ribs. Laboured rasps rattled from Corrina's punctured lungs. The pigman turned and walked to the car. Her pleas were drowned in the frothy blood gurgling over her torn lips.

CEREAL PANSY

"How much longer, Mrs Donna?" squeaked a girl's voice from behind Janie's seat.

The counsellor peered up from jotting notes on the pages of an itinerary splayed open across her lap. "At least another hour, Renée."

"But I'm sooooo bored," Renée whined. She kicked at the back of Janie's seat.

"Just be a good girl and finish colouring in your book, Renée. If you sit quietly, you won't bother anybody, and we'll soon be there."

"I'll bother who I want." Renée got up and squeezed into the vacant seat beside Janie. Janie didn't want to talk to anyone and pressed herself harder against the window. She turned her head away and stared out at the endless trees bordering foreboding towers of rock. Renée enfolded Janie's hand then snuggled up to her. "You're very bony. I can feel your ribs."

Janie yanked her hand free. Her palm was smeared with peanut butter. She snatched a handkerchief from her pocket and rubbed off the gooey mess, her heart racing a mile a minute. Janie knew calories could be absorbed through the skin, and peanut butter had ninety-four calories per tablespoon. It had to be removed quickly otherwise she'd get fat. She turned to the girl and looked into deep-set, bovine eyes that slanted upward. Bobbed red hair framed a small head with a button nose and two tiny, pink lips smeared in food paste. The girl obviously had Down syndrome. Pinned to her yellow raincoat was a large tag decorated with glitter and gold stars which stated 'Hey, hey, I'm Renée.'

"You got peanut butter all over my hand," Janie said, meticulously inspecting each finger from knuckle to chewed nail.

Renée checked her own hand for clumps of peanut butter and licked off whatever she could find. "Are you going to the camp too?"

"We all are, aren't we? That's why we're on the same bus."

Renée stared blankly at Janie and shrugged her shoulders. For the first time since she was picked up from the residential home, Janie glanced around the interior of the bus. Her eyes settled on a young man with an ashen complexion slumped in a side-facing seat in front of her. He wore an orange T-shirt much too big for his skinny frame. Thick-rimmed glasses, with even thicker lenses magnifying his eyes to the size of saucers, perched precariously on the end of his aquiline nose. The crotch of the boy's white linen trousers bulged aggressively. "Does that boy have an erection?" Janie whispered.

"That's John. He's got cereal pansy, and it makes his magic wand always hard and cry milk."

"I think you mean cerebral palsy," Janie said, her eyes still locked on the enormous erection. She politely dropped her gaze, but her eyes swiveled up again. She'd never seen one so big before.

John suddenly raised his bobbing head and glowered at the girl staring at him. "Stop looking at my cock, you pedo." John slapped his boner as if it were an obstinate child. "Fucking stiffy cunt. I hate you."

Donna reached over and grabbed his flailing wrist. "Shhhh, calm down, John. You're getting worked up again. You'll only be pumping more blood to your penis if your heart rate increases."

John scowled. "Shut up. What would you know anyway? You're a whore. Your mother is a whore. That girl over there is a whore." Janie blushed and looked away. "All girls are whores."

"We both live in Kimberly House," Renée interjected. "It's a special home. Mrs Donna says it's a place for people who have been attacked with sex."

"Like victims of sexual assault?" Janie asked.

Renée picked her nose. "I know how to use the stove. I can make pancakes. When Mrs Donna comes to visit us, she's our counsellor, you know, she always eats six pancakes." Renée reclined back in her seat and smiled proudly. The only other teen on the bus was wedged into a corner with headphones buried in his ears and his gangly legs stretched down the aisle. He sported a long emo fringe and a face full of metal.

"Are we the only people going to the camp? I thought there would be more," Janie said.

"There were two other girls coming, but they got very sick. John said it was my pancakes that made them ill."

Janie made a mental note never to eat anything Renée cooked, not that she needed any more reasons to avoid food. She hardly had an appetite. The care assistants at the residential home ensured she drank calorie-laden, high-protein smoothies three times a day. Only when she was locked in the toilet, her fingers lodged in her throat and searching for the sweet spot that heaved up the puréed meal, did she relax and feel in control of her life again.

Donna snapped shut her notebook and glanced out of the window. She mumbled something to herself, rose from her seat, and staggered toward the bus driver. The counsellor gripped his headrest and bent down low enough for the grizzled man to hear her speak. Janie strained to listen. Donna tapped her watch. "We were meant to be there an hour ago, Garrett."

"Those two girls we had to take home made us late," Garrett grunted. "So now we're an hour behind schedule."

She waved her notebook at him. "Well, that's what I wanted to talk to you about. I plotted out the route in advance, and I recall from the map there's a turning coming up that will save us at least thirty minutes."

"Best to stick to the main highway. I don't know the back roads around here. We'd be liable to get turned around and tangled up in all sorts of ways. We don't want to get lost this far out in the country."

"It's a simple route to the camp, Garrett. You take the turn and drive in a straight line all the way."

"Yeah, but Savage—"

"Garrett, we have to reach the campsite before it's completely dark, otherwise we will be putting up tents and making dinner under torchlight. I am telling you to take the next turning so we can make up some lost time and get to where we need to be before the sun goes down."

Garrett muttered under his breath, and his sturdy forearms, adorned with green blotches of tattoo ink, tightened on the large steering wheel. Janie couldn't quite hear, but she suspected he did not agree with the counsellor's demands by the way he shook his head after Donna sat down again, a triumphant look plastered over her face.

A battered wooden post with a lopsided sign pointed to a narrow side road. Garrett changed gear, and the bus jolted onto the dirt track. The trees were denser and scratched against the bus windows as the vehicle rattled along. Dwindling rays of faint sunlight broke through the scudding clouds but did little to dispel the gloom. Janie watched the perpetual line of trees blur past her as the bus jerked and juddered over the bumpy ground. Droplets of rain pattered against the window. Renée was humming a song out of tune. Janie's eyelids felt weighty and began to droop.

***

Night fell almost unnoticed, and Janie couldn't see far beyond the twisted length of barbed wire fence bordering the roadside. Distant lights shone beyond the row of trees, their trunks gnarled and bowed. *There must be a farmhouse out there*, she thought. The incessant tapping of rain on glass and metal had lulled most of the passengers to sleep. Renée, her head nestled on Janie's shoulder, snored quietly.

A huge bang shattered the calm, and the bus lurched across to the far side of the road. Tree branches pounded the windows and roof as Garrett slammed his foot on the brakes and jerked the wheel in one direction and then the other. Renée, startled awake, grabbed Janie's knee. A bolt of pain shot up Janie's leg, and she tried to tear away the girl's vice-like hold.

John let out a piercing wail as he was thrown from his side-seat to the floor. The tyres screeched, and the bus skidded and shuddered violently before smashing through the fence of spiked wire and coming to a halt in a ditch. Donna rushed to John and offered him her hand. "Is everyone alright?" she asked.

"I'm not alright, you fucking moron," John barked as he was eased back into his seat. "My prick smashed into the floor, head first. I swear I heard it fucking snap."

Donna admonished him instantly. "Watch how you speak, John. I don't approve of coarse language regardless of the circumstances."

"Oh, get fucked, saggy tits," John replied.

Donna turned toward Garrett. "What the heck happened? Did we hit something?"

"I don't know. I'll have to go and check it out." Garrett popped the door mechanism and unfolded himself out of his chair. A blast of cold air and rain shot into the bus as he stepped out.

Renée sobbed. "Are you hurt?" Janie asked, rubbing her sore knee.

"No," she snivelled. "I'm hungry." Renée rummaged around in the backpack stored between her feet and pulled out a chocolate bar. Janie peered over her headrest. The emo kid still sat in the same position, headphones and fringe undisturbed. Janie rubbed the condensation from the window and peered out into the darkness. Garrett squatted in the mud, inches away from her. He manipulated something out of the tyre, held it up, and examined it. A large rusty nail. It was soon joined by several more.

A cold eel squirmed in Janie's gut. Uninvited bile surged to the rear of her throat, and she fought hard to swallow it down. Garrett walked around the bus and booted the other tyres. He kicked viciously at another nail on the road and stepped back onto the bus, his bald pate beaded with rain and the shoulders of his coat already wet through. Donna pounced on Garrett as soon as he entered. Her high-pitched voice betrayed her concern. "Well?" she said. "What's wrong?"

Garrett ran a hand over his head and flopped down in his chair. "Four flat tyres," he sighed.

"You can change them, right?" Donna straightened her gold-rimmed spectacles which lay askew across her cheekbones.

Garrett stroked the long handlebars of his grey moustache, tinged golden from years of tobacco smoke. "No bus carries four spares."

Donna's posture slackened. John folded his arms and huffed. "Fucking great. And just when I thought nothing could be worse than spending a weekend camping with a bunch of cunts and retards. I missed a *Star Trek* marathon for this."

"How do all four bus tyres puncture simultaneously?" Janie piped up.

"Rusty nails scattered over the road will do it every time," Garrett replied.

"So, what are we going to do? Shall we call a mechanic? The police?" Donna asked, withdrawing her phone from her backpack. She tapped the screen. Then she tapped it again. And again. "I don't understand. I charged my phone this morning. Now there's no battery."

Renée stopped chomping on her chocolate bar and leaned over to Janie. "Why would there be rusty nails all over the road?" she asked. "Isn't that dangerous?"

Janie shrugged.

"Try Matt's phone," John said. He pointed to the quiet shape tucked away on the last row of seats. All eyes turned.

Matt withdrew the headphones from his ears. "Huh?" he said.

"It's an emergency. We need to use your phone. Stop listening to that shouty crap and give it to Donna," John demanded.

Matt shrugged and passed it to Donna who examined it. She tapped in a number and held the device to her ear. No one spoke while she waited for someone on the line to answer. The hand which clutched the phone fell to her side. "There's only… static. Maybe it's a weak signal. The mountains must be causing it or the trees perhaps." John clenched his fist and took out his ire on the window glass. Donna didn't attempt to stop him. "I suggest we wait here and hope a car comes along soon," Donna said. "As long as we stay on the bus, we'll be fine."

LITTLE JONOKUCHI

"When we get to the camp, can we roast marshmallows on the fire? Do you have any marshmallows?" Renée asked.

"No," Janie said.

"It's okay. I have lots." Renée opened her backpack. It was stuffed with packets of white and pink marshmallows. "I like the pink ones the best because I'm a girl." She grabbed a packet, and her cow eyes beamed as she turned the bag over excitedly in her hands.

Outside, the clouds blotted out the pale moon. Darkness pressed against the cold glass, and wind-lashed, twisted, black branches scraped along the bus. Janie stretched her hood over her eyes. The rain drumming on the metal roof helped to drown out Renée's voice. Janie knew Renée meant well. The disabled girl was harmless and friendly enough, but this weekend therapy trip into the wilderness was already proving to be overwhelming with the constant chatter and presence of other people, and they hadn't even arrived at the campsite yet. She wondered if she'd made a mistake by agreeing to participate in such an excursion. Maybe she wasn't ready after all.

For the last year, Janie had been living in a unit for teenagers with eating disorders. Stony-faced care assistants force-fed her, sometimes through a long, transparent tube, and an endless stream of doctors, nurses, and her parents monitored her every move. Her mind drifted back over the last few months.

Janie strained, and a turd that looked like an emaciated earthworm slithered down into the toilet bowl. Her parents peered between her legs. Janie placed her hands over her vagina. "Mom, Dad, do you have to watch me? Can't I have any privacy?" she said.

"You know why we have to do this, my little Jonokuchi," her father said. He handed her a strip of toilet paper.

"We just want you to get better. Now, be a good girl and eat some more chankonabe," Janie's mother said, forcing another large spoonful of steaming stew into Janie's mouth. Her father looked down at her and smiled fondly as she wiped her ass and tried to swallow the stew without gagging.

Janie shuddered at the memory. Like Renée, her parents meant well, but they were stifling. Mr and Mrs Hashimoto wanted their little Jonokuchi as she used to be, plump and well-rounded, not a ninety-pound skeleton whose fingers were down her throat after every meal. She wondered if the other kids on the bus were just as screwed up as her. Renée had survived sexual assault and seemed to be coping okay. John too had been a victim, but he obviously had anger issues. Janie glanced behind at Matt. He stared directly ahead; his eyes were as blank and grey as mushrooms. He'd rolled up his sleeves, and his remorseless fingers worried his forearms. The tattooed skin was crisscrossed with ugly, purple scars, some as thick as fettuccine. Janie had known cutters in the hospital, mostly girls who scratched at themselves with razors and posted the photos in edgy social media groups. They had nothing on Matt. What would drive someone to do something so extreme to themselves?

Donna glanced up from a thick paperback and scowled at John as he scrawled the word CUNT in huge letters on the steamy window with his finger.

"That's disgusting, John. Rub it out this instant. You know I can't abide that word."

"Fuck off," John said and added four exclamation points.

Garrett sat silently, facing the entrance to the bus, his arms folded across his chest. His mud-encrusted boots rested on a battered, canvas rucksack. Janie thought he looked like an old guard on sentry duty. His brow was creased, and his steely eyes stared unblinkingly at the closed door.

"What the fuck's taking so long? I want to get off the goddamn bus," John said, slamming his body against the padded backrest of his seat.

"You can't, John, not yet," Donna replied. "You're going to have to wait like everyone else. I suspect someone will be along eventually." She checked her wristwatch. "We've only been waiting an hour."

"I want to get off now. Get me my wheelchair, bitch."

"No, John. We stay on the bus where it's safe, and we wait for assistance. Would you like another sandwich?"

John thrashed his pencil-thin arms around and banged his head against the window glass. "Shove those sandwiches in your old, stinking, rat-infested snatch, you whore. I want my fucking wheelchair!" His fists pounded on his bony legs, then he tried to push himself up off his seat with his feeble arms. "Get me my fucking wheelchair. I want it, you cunt boil!" Donna dropped her book and lurched forward to restrain him. The angry boy wailed and whined as he lashed out at the counsellor desperately trying to clutch at his frantic limbs.

"Calm down, John, please." Donna clasped his wrists and rubbed her thumbs over the cold skin. "Relax. Breathe in slowly then exhale."

He spat a glob of thick, bubbly phlegm in Donna's face. She released her grip and wiped the spittle from her cheek. "Get me my wheelchair! I fucking hate you, you rapist cunt!" John reached out to throttle Donna. She sidestepped and batted away his scrabbling hands.

"John, no!" screamed Renée. She threw her packet of marshmallows to Janie, rushed down the aisle, and grabbed at his arm.

"You can fuck off too, you fat, ugly, mongoloid twat." John's flailing arms struck Renée in the face. The blow was no worse than a slap from a fish, but Renée burst into tears and stumbled back up the aisle. Janie had just moved the packet of marshmallows to the neighbouring seat when Renée dropped down beside her. She buried her head in the crook of Janie's arm, snuggled into her, and sobbed.

"This isn't working," Garrett said, standing up. "Nobody is going to come to our rescue." Everyone but Matt looked at him gravely, even Donna who was cleaning the spit from her glasses. "We're all clearly fed-up with waiting in the hope a car will come by. So, I'll head back to those lights we passed earlier and see whether I can get some help. Someone obviously lives out here. It's possible they'll have a phone." Garrett unzipped his rucksack and pulled out a torch. "The rest of you just stay here on the bus until I return. I mean it. Don't leave. It's not a safe place to go wandering off, especially in the dark." Garrett pressed the release button, and the door swung open.

Without saying a word, Matt sidled down the aisle and stepped out into the pouring rain and the all-engulfing darkness.

"Wait for me. I'm coming too," Janie called out. She was desperate to escape the tense atmosphere. It was suffocating her.

"If Janie's going, so am I," Renée said, clinging to Janie's arm as she struggled to stand up.

"I'm not staying on the bus alone with Donna. She'll rape me again," John said.

"Don't be revolting, John. I've just about had enough of you." Donna's face flushed with anger.

"It's better if you and Donna stay here with all our stuff until we return with help," Garrett said.

"Or when someone eventually comes along," Donna added.

Garrett rolled his eyes. "Yeah, well good luck with that." He turned to the others. "Mind where you step, ladies."

"I think you should take a couple of sandwiches for the journey," Donna said. "Here you go, Janie." She thrust the squashed bread stack wrapped in cellophane at the girl. The sandwiches were stuffed with folds of beige-coloured meat. Janie flinched and dodged backward, butting Renée in the chin with the back of her head, and knocking the tearful girl onto the top step.

"I'm really not hungry." Janie bent down to help Renée to her feet. "I don't want them."

John sniggered as Janie apologised to Renéc and struggled to lift her up.

"I'll take them, Mrs Donna," Renée said as she rubbed her chin, already beginning to swell. She snatched the sandwiches from Donna's grasp and slid them into the side pocket of her yellow raincoat. Garrett ushered Janie and Renée out of the bus and followed them into the pelting downpour.

A tempest raged as they trudged away from the stranded vehicle. Janie shivered as the wind swirled around her; the lashing rain felt like pins pricking at her skin. Water soaked through her hoodie and T-shirt, and mud sloshed around and over her sneakers. She followed the silhouettes of Garrett and Matt a few yards ahead of them. The light of a single beam oscillated along the murky ground and illuminated their precarious path. Renée clung tightly to her bicep. Janie clenched her jaw and hauled the deadweight through the mud. Pain tingled through her teeth where frequent vomiting had cracked and eroded the enamel. Janie turned her head and glanced at the bus. John stared at her from the window. His bespectacled eyes were magnified to double their normal size, and his mouth was arched in a grimace.

SPASTIC COCK

The darkness swallowed up the light from Garrett's torch. John scraped at the long, thin crescent of snot smeared on the window glass with his fingernail. He looked past the nasal mucus at the eerie forest landscape. A white flash of lightning momentarily lit up the black sky, followed by the ominous rumble of thunder.

"Come back from the window, Johnny. We'll be here alone for a long time." The harsh tone Donna had used to admonish him earlier for his unruly behaviour had softened to a persuasive lilt.

John shuddered. He couldn't believe he'd ended up alone with this bitch. He hated Donna and all the other women who treated him like a piece of meat. His mouth was parched, and he swallowed hard. "No. I'll keep watch until they return."

"Don't be such a stick in the mud. We can have some fun to pass the time."

John turned his head around slowly, and his worse fears were confirmed. Donna had stripped herself of her blouse and bra. Her pallid breasts hung down like two overladen saddle bags, the areolas a deep shade of purple. She pinched and twisted a rubbery nipple with her meaty fingers. John's eyes narrowed and the corners of his lips turned down as the fingers slowly dropped to her thighs, and she hitched up her skirt. Black, spider-leg pubes sprouted from the sides of her white, lacy panties. Donna pulled aside her underwear to reveal a dark bush, as wild and tangled as the flora surrounding the bus.

"Do you like what you see, Johnny? I know you do. My Johnny boy can't get enough of Mummy's sweet, succulent pussy." Donna purred and chewed on her bottom lip. She ran her hands slowly over her flabby, stretch-marked belly and then across her pale, dimpled thighs as if she were ironing out the creases.

"Don't come near me. You're revolting. You look like an uncooked dumpling," John scowled. He scrunched up his face and puffed out his chest to appear big and brave, but inside he felt small and wanted to cry. Ever since he was a little boy, life had been like this. John's cock, a veritable meat feast, stood out like Gulliver in Lilliput. It was also rock hard twenty-four seven. Women couldn't keep their hands off it. They saw only his penis and not the tortured, crippled, young man it was attached to.

John couldn't blame them, though, for wanting to fuck him. His dick was magnificent, thirteen and three-quarter inches uncut, with the girth of a beer can, and wrapped up in pulsing, thick veins that would make a bodybuilder weep with jealousy. John looked like Billy Idol too, if Billy had had muscular dystrophy and his father had been a retarded goat. He wouldn't mind if he got some kind of satisfaction from sex. The problem was his twisted spine. Despite giving him a perpetual boner, the trapped nerves had also totally desensitized it. John could drive nails through his prick and not blink. It was fucking tragic. He was blessed with a one-in-a-billion cock and a daily stream of pussy and ass throwing itself at him. It would have been fair, and a much-welcomed distraction from living in the mangled freak show of the body he was born with, to allow him, at the very least, to enjoy his sought-after cock too. But no, the powers that be decided he would be dead from the waist down.

Donna was the greediest sex fiend of them all. Their counselling sessions had degenerated into hardcore fuck fests from the first time she had laid her eyes on his irresistible pole. She lifted a chubby, short leg, put her foot on the seat beside him, and parted her beefy flaps so John could see into her dripping, gaping hole. "See what you do to me with that big, hard cock of yours, Johnny boy? I've been aching to ride it since we left the care home this morning. But the others wouldn't like that, would they? They'd get jealous, and I want your cock all to myself. I don't want to share it with that skinny, bulimic bitch or the gluttonous retard." Donna strummed her vaginal lips with her finger, making her creamy cunt look like Steven Tyler blowing a raspberry while eating cottage cheese.

"You can't have it." John threw himself to the ground and dragged himself to his wheelchair.

"Remember our little agreement, John. You play nice or Mummy gets out the 'certified insane' stamp, and you'll spend the rest of your days as Bedlam Mental Health Asylum's fuck toy."

That was the last thing John wanted. "Okay, but no anal this time."

"I told you that wasn't my fault. I'd been to an all-you-can-eat Chinese buffet for lunch and needed to make room."

John shuddered at the memory. Donna flipped him over and expertly unbuttoned his trousers with one hand as she fingered herself with the other. John's cock sprang out to greet her despite his protestations. Donna's legs quivered in anticipation. She straddled him and pinned his skinny arms above his head. John stared up at her through the thick lenses of his glasses.

"Be gentle," John pleaded. His prick rested on his belly, the tip reaching his sternum. Donna drooled like a bloodhound on the scent.

"Foreplay first, Johnny boy." Donna yanked down John's trousers and ground her sopping pussy hard against his withered, bony thigh. She groaned in ecstasy. A snail trail of arousal juice glistened from his knee to his pelvis. John winced and tears streamed down his face as she polished her grape-like clit over his skin.

Donna removed John's glasses, scooted up and squatted over his face. She spread her labia and fucked his nose. John gasped for breath. His weak lungs couldn't suck in enough air as his lips bounced rhythmically off her asshole. Her pungent musk filled his nostrils, and he tasted a cornucopia of bitter flavours sprinkled with stray pubic hairs. Panicking, John sucked at her anus. Donna moaned in pleasure and rode his face harder. Flappy meat filled the well between John's teeth, and he chomped down hard. "Ooooh, that's it, Johnny boy, right there!"

Donna slid down his chest and belly and guided his throbbing member into her loose hole. "Oooh, that's lovely, Johnny boy. That's just bliss. Give it to Mummy nice and deep. Mmm, such a good little runt. That solid, spastic cock is so big it fills me right up." She jammed every inch of John's rigid phallus into her hungry sex.

"You nearly suffocated me," John blubbered. He was half-blind, and his face was sticky with pussy and anal secretions. While he wept, her juices bubbled from his nostrils.

"Stop complaining. There are worse ways to die." Donna slammed her cunt down and tugged at her acorn-sized nipples. John wailed like a newborn as the sound of his ball sack slapping Donna's asshole echoed throughout the bus. "F-f-fuck, I'm about to cum." Donna flung back her head and screamed as she edged closer to a climax.

A large, dark shape drifted past the window. "I think maybe the others are coming back," John whimpered. He prayed it was the others. He begged silently to be saved from this sexual assault.

Donna's slack jaw snapped shut, and her eyeballs rolled down as she scanned the darkness surrounding the bus. Something passed the window again and moved nearer the door. "Shit." Donna jumped up and clasped her pendulous breasts. John's slick, frothy cock slapped onto his belly. The door rattled and shook.

"Just a minute." Donna scrabbled around on the floor, picked up her clothes, and hastily dressed. She hoisted up John's trousers, handed him his glasses, and glared menacingly at him, her index finger pressed to her lips. John nodded in acquiescence. He knew no one would believe him if he claimed to have been coerced into sex by his counsellor. In the past, the people he'd confided in had molested him too or said he had a bad attitude and deserved it. His anger was his coping mechanism for the endless violations he was subjected to. She smoothed down her skirt, and patting her hair, shuffled bowlegged toward the door.

John wiped the crust from his lips and the tears from his eyes then hauled himself up onto his shaky arms. He watched as Donna pressed the release button next to Garrett's seat. Donna turned and screamed. An arm knotted with muscle thrust through the doorway, seized her by the throat, and dragged her into the rain. John clutched at the seat and pulled himself up high enough to see through the window. He stared open-mouthed at the towering shape. It craned its head up to the blackened sky, grunting and snorting. Mist spurted from its rounded, flat nose like a geyser with each exhalation. "That man has the head of… the head of… a fucking pig!" John gasped.

Donna squirmed helplessly on the ground until her tormentor raised his boot and stomped on her back. The crack echoed through the trees, and her body concaved at the waist. No cry followed the attack, only violent retching as blood filled Donna's throat. John hadn't noticed the sledgehammer until the pigman dropped it beside the gurgling counsellor. It splashed in a large puddle of muddy water.

John clasped both hands over his mouth to stop himself from crying out. The pigman grabbed Donna's head and yanked it back. John flinched as the sound of muscle being torn from bone rose above the ceaseless drumming of rain on the bus roof overhead. Twisting the head around so she faced the sky, the pigman planted his huge boot on Donna's shoulder and ripped the skull free. A blistering snap and it came away in his hand. The blood spray shot several feet from the open neck. The spinal cord followed and dangled like a coaxial cable in his hand. John gawped as Donna's eyelids fluttered, and her mouth twitched as if she were trying to speak her last words.

The pigman flung Donna's head down and turned his attention to the bus. Another clap of thunder startled John as he glanced at the pigman's hideous face. "Oh fuck," John mouthed. He hunkered down below the window, his heart pounding in his chest. "Oh fuck, oh fuck, oh fuck." He could try to close the door, but he doubted he would make it in time, and besides, that thing looked as if he could rip the bus apart with his bare hands. John gripped his erect cock. If the pigman were to see how well-hung John was too, there was no telling what he would do to him. His only choice was to hide and hope the pigman didn't know he was onboard.

John slid to the floor and wiggled into the gap under the side seat. He buried himself behind some plastic carrier bags belonging to Donna. The floor vibrated as the pigman stormed into the bus. John peeked through a hole and saw two very large, worn, leather boots thud past, accompanied by a sudden outburst of high-pitched, nasally squeals. John shrank further back against the wall, holding his breath.

INBRED WEIRDO

The dirt road stretched on endlessly. Only the bobbing light from Garrett's torch was visible ahead. Crooked tree limbs bent from both sides of the road to form an archway that blocked out the sky. Janie thought they looked like scrawny fingers interlocked. It was as if nature herself harboured some malevolent intent to keep Janie engulfed in the shadows. She shuddered and pulled her rain-soaked hood tight. The lightning became more frequent, and the thunder sounded as if it were creeping nearer. "I don't like this place," Renée said. "It's spooky." She huddled in closer to Janie.

Garrett stepped with the caution and alertness of an old soldier tasked with being on point and guiding his tentative troops through an unfamiliar, hostile terrain. All four of them were drenched to the bone, but no one voiced their discomfort. Finding the farmhouse was too important.

As the rain swept in through the gaps in the canopy, Janie cursed herself for having agreed to this trip, and she cursed Donna for having persuaded her. Anxiety bubbled up inside her empty stomach. Every step forward was like wading through slowly drying concrete. She wanted to go back to the sanctuary of the stranded bus. Shielding her eyes, she stared over her shoulder, hoping to catch a glimpse of the vehicle's distant lights. The road behind had vanished into a void, a blackness so complete that her heart thudded against her ribs.

The wind drilled into her bones, making them ache and freezing them to the marrow. She'd never known such cold. To push ahead and find the farmhouse was the only option now, so she pressed on in Garrett's and Matt's wake. Exhausted, Janie dragged Renée along in silence. Her head ached, her legs were filled with lead, and her brain was foggy. She hadn't kept down a proper meal or exercised in months—she hadn't done much of anything except vomit and sleep—and they lagged behind.

Garrett turned around and waited for the girls to catch up. He shone the beam of light directly into their faces. "Come on, ladies. I'm sure it's just around this next bend."

Janie gritted her teeth and quickened her pace. They rounded a curve in the road, and the dense cluster of trees opened up. A hazy glow slipped through the narrow breaks between the tree trunks. The four wanderers followed a rusty barbed wire fence and caught glimpses of an overgrown field through the tree line, a swaying sea of stalks barely visible through the downpour. The fence stopped at an unlatched cattle gate, swinging open from the force of the wind. A ceaseless moan of creaking hinges cut through the rain. Garrett held the gate firmly against the wind and traced the metallic frame with his torchlight. It settled on a badly dented sign bolted to the panel. Renée read aloud the illuminated words slowly, pointing to each word in turn: 'TRESSPASSERS WILL BE'. She stopped. The rest of the sign was too damaged to decipher.

Janie strained her eyes to see beyond the gate. From atop a steep hill, a large ramshackle farmhouse stared down at them. A ghostly mass of grey smoke curled from its chimney stack. The winding dirt driveway was a graveyard of abandoned farm equipment. Long grass wove through the broken tractors and rusty pickup trucks like the tentacles of a kraken, dragging down helpless ships to their watery fate. Garrett held open the gate for the others. He led the way along the track, followed closely by Matt. They slogged along up the uneven ground cratered with pot holes and choked with weeds until they could see dust-speckled light through the grimy windows, revealing peeled wallpaper, weathered wood, and crumbling masonry.

By the time they reached the hilltop, Janie was puffing, and her legs threatened to give way. The distorted shrubbery and thick weeds surrounding the house had conquered the porch. Jungle-like vines circled the railings, wound their way through the floorboards, and snared Janie's and Renée's wet feet as they plodded up the rotten wood steps. A creeping plant was tangled around the rails on a rocking chair, the seat tilted forward as if it had been captured mid motion. "I wonder who lives here?" Renée asked. Janie shrugged. She was just grateful to be out of the rain. Her clothes were sodden. Water had soaked through her sneakers and socks, and she couldn't wait to remove them.

"Remember, people are different out here. They aren't used to outsiders like us," Garrett said. He turned off the torch, opened the tattered flyscreen, and rapped on the front door. Janie held her breath and strained to listen for approaching footfalls above the sound of the rain thrumming on the porch roof. Thunder boomed.

Heavy footsteps echoed from the bowels of the house and clomped down a long corridor. The front door swung open, and the stench of refuse wafted out. An elderly woman with blue curlers jutting from her hair grinned at them. She looked the newcomers up and down, her gaze lingering on Matt the longest. She wiped her large, raw-knuckled hands over a coarse work apron covering a faded yellow sundress, staining it with brown streaks.

"Who be this that's callin' in on us at such a late 'our?" the woman croaked.

"We don't mean to disturb you," Garrett said apologetically. "Our bus broke down a way back, and we're hoping you have a phone we could use."

"Phone, you say? No phone 'ere. Never 'ad no need for such a thing." Her smile widened, showing a row of corn kernel teeth. She sized Garrett up for a moment. "But ma boy will be 'ome soon, not long ta be waitin' now. He 'as a tow truck. Will getcha back on the road, good as new. Come in an' wait."

Garrett peered past her at the rubbish-strewn corridor. "We wouldn't want to be any trouble, thank you. We can wait here for your son."

The woman laughed, a maniacal sound like a gurgling plughole. "Nonsense. Come in outta the wet an' the cold. Name's Mama Dolores. Pleasure ta make ye acquaintance."

"Thank you. I'm Garrett. This is Matt, Janie and Renée."

Mama Dolores' attention shifted across to the skinny girl shivering on her porch. "Janie's a pretty name, so it is. I 'ad a Bentheim Black Pied pig called Janie. Was a good sow, sturdy 'til 'er final days. Then ma boy 'ad ta take a sledgehammer ta 'er 'ead 'cause she couldn't bear fruit, so ta speak."

"Thank you, I think," Janie said taking off her dripping hoodie and hanging it over the rail of the rocking chair. She bent over to remove her shoes.

"Don't ye be a-fussin' about removin' no shoes. Now, who'd be that retard a-'idin', behind ye?"

"This is Renée," Garrett said and removed his damp, khaki fishing vest.

Renée peeped out from behind Janie and held out her hand. "Hi, I'm Renée. I like to make pancakes."

"Ain't never 'ad a pig called Renée. Would've bashed its brains in if I 'ad, that I would."

Renée disappeared behind Janie again.

"Folla me." Mama Dolores turned and waddled along the corridor into the mire of filth. Janie and Renée followed Matt and Garrett inside. Janie gagged from the stench invading her nostrils and had to make a concerted effort to breathe only through her mouth. The acrid taste of phantom rotten meat and vegetables burnt her throat.

The smell grew worse as they moved along the corridor. A greenish smog hung in the air. What Janie thought was the hum of an air conditioner was the buzz of flies. As they trod carefully over the scattered debris, the flies rose in dense, black clouds and dinged against her skin like pellets of hail. Rubbish crunched and squelched beneath their muddy shoes. The few visibly bare floorboards were a grubby, indistinct colour that matched the dingy, smeared wallpaper. A dry, crusty film covered every surface.

Janie peered into several rooms packed full with junk and long closed off from sunlight by grime-coated curtains. In one room, a mannequin with its face chipped away was surrounded by a ring of broken tricycles. In another room, Janie thought she saw a small, pale face beneath a grand piano veiled in many years of dust and cobwebs, but when she looked again, the face had disappeared.

"This is quite the place you've got here," Garrett said.

Mama Dolores stopped and turned around, halting her four new guests in their tracks. "This place 'as been in ma family for more generations than ye can count, so it 'as," Mama Dolores said proudly. "We be some of the first settlers of Savage River. Ye could even say the river's in our blood, yessir."

"It has a certain reputation," Garrett said. Mama Dolores looked at him, eyebrow raised. "I mean among superstitious people, that's all."

"Does it now? I wouldn't know nothin' 'bout that." Mama Dolores continued along the corridor and flung open the final door at the end of the hall.

A foul reek wafted out. Overwhelmed, Janie pressed the sleeve of her shirt to her nose. In the centre of the room was a long wooden table laden with dirty dishes and encrusted pots. Fat blowflies cruised above the putrefying banquet.

"Just go an' pull up a seat at that 'ere table. I'll fix somethin' ta eat while ye wait."

"You needn't worry. We ate on the bus," Garrett said.

"And I have sandwiches," Renée said, dipping her hand into her pocket.

"Shush. This 'ere child be nothin' more than skin and bone," she said, pinching Janie's arm. "She needs a proper 'omecooked meal, she does." Mama Dolores bustled out of the room and into the adjacent kitchen. Janie rubbed the spot on her arm where Mama Dolores had nipped her. She dreaded to think what the conditions were like behind that door. She remembered seeing a black and white photograph of Ed Gein wearing his lumber jack hat and squatting in his squalid kitchen. The murderer had dismembered his corpses among the filth and decay and fashioned them into grisly trophies. The photo still haunted her. Janie realised she had been holding her breath and was forced to inhale.

"Maybe she's cooking pancakes. I better go and help her," Renée said.

"Sit down, Renée," Garrett said, pointing to the chair beside him.

"Fuck, this place is filthy." Matt shoved a plate of decomposing leftovers away from him as he sat down next to Renée.

"Just ignore it. We don't have to eat anything. We're here until the son can help us with his tow truck," Garrett said.

Janie pinched her nostrils and peered into the once-silver pot beside her. Bones stuck out from the black congealed substance coating the base. She looked away and glanced around the rest of the table. A thick layer of mould grew over torn chunks of stale bread, and maggots writhed in meat scraps left to spoil on greasy dishes.

"The old woman is obviously an inbred weirdo. Her son is most likely also her brother and her husband," Matt said.

"That's mean, Matt," Renée said and patted his arm.

Seated in a strange house among decomposing food, Janie experienced the stirring of familiar symptoms. Her heart fluttered, her brow moistened, and her fingers tingled. She was on the verge of a freakout. Hearing a soft whimper, Garrett turned to Janie. "What? You don't like country life then?"

Janie hugged herself and let out a high-pitched giggle at the absurdity of Garrett's comment. The dining room door was kicked open and Mama Dolores, haloed by a cloud of steam, entered. Her hands were clenched around the handle of a large cauldron, and she breathed heavily from the sheer weight of it.

Garrett stood up to help, but Mama Dolores waved him down with a shake of her head and thumped the heavy pot onto the table. The vibration set the plates and pots rattling and flung the maggots into the air like contorting trapeze artists. She shoved four grubby bowls under her guests' noses and spooned in large portions of grey mince swimming in an opaque, watery broth.

Janie fought the bitter bile surging up her throat as she watched clumps of mince bubble in her dish. She couldn't stand the sight of the sludge let alone the thought of eating it. Glancing over at the others, Janie knew they suffered similarly from the looks on their faces.

"Thank you, it looks delicious," Garrett said through gritted teeth.

"It's an ol' family recipe." Mama Dolores' huge hands closed around her own overflowing bowl of mince, and she raised it to her lips. Her throat bobbed up and down as she drained it. Sloppy rivulets streamed from the sides of her mouth, adding another layer of grime to the stained apron.

Matt paled and looked at Renée who was frowning down at her bowl. Janie poked at her food with a spoon and covered her mouth as a solid piece of hairy gristle floated to the surface, and an unwholesome effluvium drifted up from the dish.

"What do you farm all the way out here?" Garrett stirred the greasy globules around in circles.

Mama Dolores belched. "Pig farmers we be," she said as she helped herself to another portion from the cauldron.

"This is supposed to be pork then?" Janie said, holding up a spoon and letting the sludge plop into the bowl.

Renée gripped Matt's arm. "What's up with you?" Matt asked.

"I don't like pigs," Renée murmured.

Mama Dolores smiled at Garrett. Morsels of mince were stuck to her stained teeth. "All our lives we be farmin' swine." She turned to Renée. "Now why would it be that ye don't be likin' pigs?"

"I... I... I just don't." Renée lowered her eyes to her steaming bowl.

Mama Dolores tilted her head and listened to the creepy silence of the house. "The rain 'as eased up now."

"How can you tell?" Janie asked, incredulous. "You can't hear it."

"I can 'ear it," Mama Dolores shot back instantly. "An' if ye live as long as we be livin' out 'ere, girl, ye get ta know 'ow this place be. Get ta know 'er patterns. Get ta know 'er signs."

"Who do you mean by 'her'?" Janie asked.

"Savage River! What are ye, an idiot child like your friend be?" She flicked her gaze to Renée. "An' the river don't take verra kindly ta strangers neither. Explains ye bus breakin' down and the storm, don't it?"

Janie flinched as something nudged her thigh. A dog, thank god. She slid the bowl from the table to her lap. Her life saver buried its nose in the bowl and slurped up the sludge. She coughed politely into her hand to cover up the sounds of slopping as Mama Dolores continued to ramble like a madwoman.

The nose nuzzled against her leg again. She peeked under the table to check if the dog had finished and was startled to see the bristled face of a large hog pressed up against her. The bowl wasn't quite empty either. Sitting at the bottom, in a shallow pool, were three strange objects, glistening and ivory coloured. Janie pinched her fingers together and retrieved one.

A molar with a filling!

Janie's stomach cramped as if absorbing a sudden punch to the gut. She pushed the chair away and jumped to her feet. "It's a human tooth!" The hog waddled out from under the table and snuffled at the floor for edible debris.

"It's a pig!" Renée screamed. Flapping her arms about wildly, she ran from the room. "I'll get her," Garrett said, racing after the flailing girl. Matt got up to leave, but Mama Dolores put a heavy hand on his shoulder and held him down.

Janie's ears pricked up as she heard the front door slam open. Mama Dolores' empty bowl clattered to the table, and the hollow sound reverberated through the kitchen. "Ma boy's 'ome," she declared, a gleam in her fiery eyes.

TWIRLING BALLERINAS

The colossal shape blocking the doorway lashed out and snatched at Renée. The girl shrieked, dashed past her towering attacker, and shouldered her way through the flyscreen. She raced down the rickety porch steps and disappeared into the night. Garrett skidded along the floor, sending up a groundswell of debris. He slammed into the pigman's broad, brawny chest, catapulted backward, and sprawled to the floor.

"What is it? What is that thing?" Janie screamed, peering from behind the doorjamb of the dining room.

"That there be ma boy. He be wantin' ta make ye acquaintance," Mama Dolores said, her hand still firmly clutching Matt's shoulder. Her mince-speckled lips curled into a malicious grin. The pigman was at least four hundred pounds of solid muscle and easily seven feet tall. His garb of oily denim overalls and work boots revealed the thick, coarse hair covering his bare arms and neck. The weak overhead light gave his skin a whitish sheen. His large snout, dripping grey mucus, dominated the abominable, porcine face. Broken tombstone teeth, crowding the lopsided mouth, gnashed and snapped menacingly.

Garrett sat up, flopped against the wall, and groggily shook his head. The pigman cast his stony, black pupils down at the man and snorted. A stream of snot shot out of his nostrils and sprayed over Garrett as he scrambled drunkenly to his feet. The pigman lumbered forward and swung a fist into Garrett's temple. He flew through the air and smashed into a hanging mirror before sliding back down the wall and crashing to the floor. Garrett spat out fragments of teeth and mouthfuls of blood as he lay writhing and groaning on the ground beside the muddy work boots.

Janie screamed again, and Mama Dolores laughed. The pigman locked eyes with the girl down the corridor. He lowered his head and charged toward her, but Garrett reached out and grabbed his leg with both hands. Janie backed into the dining room, knocking over a tower of dirty plates and saucepans stacked precariously on the table.

Matt swiped at Mama Dolores' flabby arm and flung back his chair. He grabbed Janie and yanked her toward the kitchen door. "We've got to get the fuck out of here now."

"Ye stayin' ta meet ma son." Mama Dolores dragged a rusty meat cleaver from the folds of her apron and scurried around the table with a speed that belied her bulk. She blocked the entrance to the kitchen and brandished the blade inches in front of Matt's chest.

Janie gasped and edged backward. "Fuck that," Matt said. "We're leaving." He batted away Mama Dolores' arm and lunged for the kitchen door handle. Mama Dolores threw all her weight into a single chop and buried the cleaver deep into his forearm. Matt yelped. He staggered back from the door and cradled his wounded arm. "You fucking bitch," he bellowed.

"That'll teach ye, swine! I'll 'ave it off next time." Matt's blood dripped down the blade onto her wrist. Janie scanned the dining room for something to defend herself with. The big pot! It still steamed with the foul concoction Mama Dolores had brewed up. She grasped the handle and hefted it up. "Want some more of Mama's 'omecookin', eh?" Mama Dolores said, shuffling toward her.

"After you." Janie threw the contents of the pot at the old woman. The stew splashed onto her chest and up into her face. Globules of hot mince clung to her reddened skin. Mama Dolores dropped the cleaver and howled. She stamped her feet and clawed at her steaming face. The pigman smashed open the door and stomped into the dining room, his mighty chest heaving. Matt and Janie darted past a screaming Mama Dolores and hurried through to the kitchen. Matt paused and snatched up the large cleaver embedded in the wooden floorboards.

The kitchen was a mire of putrefaction. Fat, chirping beetles crawled over the cluttered surfaces. Long-abandoned saucepans and plates lazed in a grease-coated porcelain sink, saturated with squirming, pulsating maggots. Clumps of pig excrement blanketed the floor. The wooden countertops were awash in dark, congealed blood. A mixing bowl next to an assortment of grub-smothered crockery held the pulpy remains of a dead baby. Janie's head swam at the grisly sight. She jammed her knuckles in her mouth and reeled back against a row of cupboards.

Matt, in pain and ashen-faced, pushed her through the back entrance.

Chilly air blasted their faces as they lurched outside and blundered into the grey mist. A row of lofty pines loomed before them, and the river roared in the distance. They ran to the trees, stumbling over the sodden ground and weaving among the mechanical refuse. Janie glanced over her shoulder and saw the pigman in the doorway, only a slither of light surrounding him. "He's coming," Janie screamed. Matt didn't look. He kept running toward the tree line, Janie's hand tight in his. She felt the warmth of his blood trickling into her palm.

The pigman pounded down the back steps and thundered behind them. A watery light glimmered from the moon, and they fled toward the concealing blackness of the woodland. The cold night air stabbed at Janie's lungs, and her wet feet sank into the mud. They'd gained in distance from their pursuer when the outline of a barn roof came into view at the edge of the trees. Fleeting shapes darted among the cluster of dense branches, and strange cries echoed in the darkness as they neared the building. Janie's skin prickled with cold and fear. Her breath came in painful gasps. "What about the others? Where did Renée go?"

Matt must have been thinking the same because his pace slowed. "I don't know, but we need to get to that barn. We can hole up there. Stumbling about in the woods without a torch and that... whatever it is out there... well, that's the worst thing we could do."

Janie couldn't see Matt's face, but from the cracks in his voice, she knew his wound hurt, and he needed to rest. She risked another look over her shoulder. The woods had swallowed them up in its shadow, and the pigman was no longer giving chase. Matt tripped and pitched forward onto his knees. Janie squatted to help him stand. His hand was sticky with blood, and his face was ghost grey. She dragged him to his feet, and with her arm around his waist, they staggered on toward the barn.

They found an unlocked side door and slipped inside. Janie snipped the latch and barred the door. Matt immediately slumped onto the hay-strewn floor. Moonbeams shone faintly through a high arched window and illuminated cross-sections of the huge barn. The air was musty with the aroma of farm animals mixed with the earthy damp of rotten wood. Janie needed to stop the blood flow from Matt's arm. She tore a strip from her shirt and tied a tourniquet around his bicep. The bleeding slowed to a trickle. "We have to find a weapon, a pitchfork, hatchet, anything to defend ourselves with," Matt said, struggling to his feet. Janie realised he wasn't holding the meat cleaver anymore. He must have dropped it somewhere in the darkness when he fell.

Together they searched the barn, Matt leaning on Janie as a crutch. An old, gutted tractor covered in years' worth of pigeon shit was parked in front of a tool bench. The tyres were flat and cables dangled from the engine hood like exposed innards. Janie searched through the rubbish on the tool bench and unearthed a wrench. Matt looked at the other discarded machines littering the barn and spotted a scythe veiled in cobwebs. "Who still uses a scythe?" Matt asked. Colour had returned to his face, but he leaned on the broken machinery for assistance. "I need something better. Maybe an axe."

Janie was starting to think it was a mistake coming into the barn. With Matt so weak and only a wrench and a scythe for protection, what chance did they have against the formidable pigman and his insane, cannibalistic mother? Surely it would be better to take their chances in the woods? Maybe they could hide there and wait until morning came, and with it, the safety of daylight. Anyhow, they were here now. The barn was locked, and if they stayed quiet, the pigman shouldn't find them. They pushed deeper into the shadows.

Something shifted in the farthest corner of the barn. A grunt and a squeal echoed from the semidarkness ahead. "Another pig?" Janie whispered.

Matt shrugged. "Sure smells like it." They crept forward, trying to avoid the animal shit piled up around their shoes.

A force charged at the barn door, rattling it on its hinges. "Fuck, he must have found us," Janie cried. The pigman repeatedly crashed into the door. The whole barn shuddered and showered Matt and Janie with dust. The door held firm, but there was no telling for how long. "What are we going to do, Matt?" There was no answer. "Matt?"

"Jesus fucking Christ," Matt gulped in response.

Janie momentarily ignored the loud thumping at the barn door and followed Matt's line of sight to the movement in the corner. A scream froze in her throat.

Tucked in the gloom, a huge sow lay on her side. Six soft, grub-like piglets writhed over her body and sucked from her swollen teats. The head of the sow was bulbous and human shaped. Long strands of straggly golden hair parted to reveal large, luminous eyes as she lifted her head. The piglets unlatched themselves from the teats and turned their deformed, human faces toward the two gawping intruders. Milk dribbled from the sow's nipples and ran down onto the bed of straw beneath her fleshy body.

"Meat, children, meat," the sow croaked.

Janie staggered back and collided into a large, bloody meat hook hanging from the rafters. Janie clutched at her hair and screamed. The barn door creaked and shuddered. The panels caved-in, and the pigman burst through in a shower of splintered wood. Matt wheeled around as the monster bounded at them like a raging bull. He swung his scythe, and the blade slashed into the pigman's head. It opened up a deep laceration but bounced off the skull.

Ignoring the gush of blood, the pigman throttled Matt, hauled him up by the throat, and slammed him down onto a meat hook. The sharp, steel point squelched through his flesh. He hung suspended in the air dripping blood. Janie wanted to run. She wanted to hide, but somehow, she found the strength inside herself to swing her wrench at the monstrosity. The blow was feeble, and it ricocheted off the beast's leathery skin without doing any damage.

The pigman slapped away the tool and grasped Janie around her scrawny arms. He hoisted up the screaming girl and shoved her onto a vacant meat hook beside Matt. Pain seared through her convulsing body. Together they twirled like ballerinas from the rafters.

Mama Dolores, her crimson face blistered and blotchy, trudged through the broken doorway. The pigman turned to his mother, his snout twitching. Through fluttering eyelids, Janie saw the sow shuffle across the straw. The piglets were dragged along beneath her, still sucking on the stretched teats. "Ah, Mama, new meat. New meat for the children, Mama," Marian said.

Mama Dolores smiled and nodded. She reached up on tiptoes to touch the blood dribbling down her son's forehead. As she switched her attention to Janie and Matt, the smile turned into a scowl. "Ah, I see ye've met ma daughter, Marian," Mama Dolores said.

TITHEADS

Renée crashed through the trees, sobbing screams rising from her throat. Her arms flailed against outstretched branches, and sharp twigs scratched her skin. Tangled roots trapped her feet and sent her stumbling to the ground.

Pigs freaked her out. A sniff of bacon triggered cold sweats, and if *Porky Pig* or *Peppa Pig* came on the television, she'd shriek and rush from the room. This pathological fear stemmed from her childhood. When she was ten, her parents had been decapitated in a grisly paddle boat accident, and she'd been sent to live with her uncle on his farm. Uncle Bob, a simple man, refused to allow her into the house. He didn't want to catch the Down syndrome, and he locked her in the pen with the pigs. The pen was spacious, warm, and comfortable, and there was always plenty of food in the trough. She enjoyed burrowing through the straw and playing hide-and-seek with the piglets until, one day, a new pig came to live at the farm.

Uncle Bob introduced the latest arrival as Boris, a nine-hundred-pound Yorkshire hog he'd bought to replace his deceased, much-loved, prized pig, Crumpet. Renée's carefree days ended then and there. Boris was a ruthless bastard. The boy piglets were bullied and brutalized, and the girls were frequently forced to accommodate the hog's carnal needs. He gobbled down most of the food and would headbutt any pig or person who dared to come near him while he was eating. The piglets spent their days cowering in fear of their new pen mate and scrounging for the morsels he'd either missed or dropped from his mouth.

Renée managed to avoid Boris, but one afternoon, as she and the piglets squabbled over a rotten potato, Boris charged into the melee and came face to face with the young girl. From that moment, Renée was his special fuck toy. Many years passed before the authorities noticed she wasn't listed on any of the schools' rolls and began to make inquiries into her absence. They finally tracked her down, but by then the physical and mental damage was already done. Renée didn't want to be within a hundred yards of a pig, or any pork products, for the rest of her life.

A warning rose up from the blind panic and ordered her to stop running. She was silly to have dashed off into the trees by herself. Aware of her surroundings for the first time, she realised she was deep in the dark, unfamiliar woods. The nearby river roared, and the wind whistled and thrashed through the branches. Mist swirled around the towering trees making them look like huge trolls. Renée shivered. Strange cries reverberated around her, and vague shapes darted among the shadows. Fear threaded through her body. Renée was more afraid of the woods now than the pig back at the farmhouse. At least Janie, Matt, and Garrett were there, whereas she was all alone here. She decided she should return to the bus. Donna and John would be happy to see her. She would tell them all about the strange, old lady who called herself 'Mama Dolores.'

A slither of moon peeked through the clouds. The trees pressing around her all looked the same, and she was unsure which way to go. The ground was a mire of soggy leaves and rotting branches, and she'd left no footprints to follow. A loud crack of snapping twigs echoed through the eerie darkness. Renée panicked and ran. Wet foliage slapped her face, and her hands and knees bled from stinging cuts as she stumbled over roots and rocks. She tumbled down a steep bank and rolled into a muddy hollow. Winded, she lay gasping and stared at the myriad of distant stars overhead. A tree branch hung just above her, and grasping it, she pulled herself up.

Renée brushed at the lumps of damp soil stuck to her clothes and hauled a foot, minus a shoe, from the suckering mud. She squatted down and was digging in the sludge when a sharp pain shot across her bottom. Renée yelped and jerked up, clasping her cheeks. A hail of projectiles launched themselves from behind the trees. Renée shielded her head with her arms as acorns pinged off her and plopped into the surrounding dirt. "Why are you trees throwing acorns at me? What have I done?" Blurry outlines moved in the undergrowth. "Is someone there?" she asked.

"Are you lost, little piggy?" a shape called out from the dark.

"Who said that? Are you a fairy?" Renée had read about mischievous fae folk playing tricks on humans that were lost in the woods. She reached into her coat pocket and pulled out the squashed sandwiches Donna had given her. "Would you like some sandwiches?"

"We're not fairies. Two more guesses," the darkness replied.

"Goblins?" she blurted out, rubbing at a particularly angry welt on her arm. She knew goblins lived in the woods and were very naughty.

"No. Last guess," a chorus of disembodied voices called out.

Renée scrunched up her face. Maybe they were horrid, little children with nothing better to do than play tricks on hapless strangers. "Children? Leprechauns?"

"Both wrong," the voices chimed.

"Who are you then?" Renée was terrified now. Maybe they were monsters. She returned the sandwiches to her pocket and pulled her coat tightly around her. A crowd of strange creatures emerged slowly from the shadows. In the dim light, Renée strained her eyes to see better. The bodies didn't look right. As they skulked toward her, Renée flinched back in fear and gasped. The shapes were a twisted amalgamation of pig and human pieces. Snouts replaced noses, and ankles sprouted trotters. Some walked upright, some crawled, and some slithered over the wet earth using nubs for limbs. There was no sense of order, and the distribution of body parts was completely random. "You're… pigrens!" Renée shrieked.

The naked mutants joined hands and trotters, forming a circle, and danced around her as if she were a maypole. They sang with whiny, distorted voices, their lips curled back over broken, jagged teeth:

"Fat little pig has got no brains,

Break her bones, wrap her in chains!

Cut her throat, peel off her face,

Fat little pig is a waste of space!"

Renée tried to barge through the ring, but they laughed and shoved her back into the middle of the swaying, revolving circle. They continued to sing:

"Fat little pig has got no friends,

Fat little pig's life must surely end!

Sharpen your knives, make her cry,

Bleed her out and watch her die!"

She clenched her jaw, and her pudgy fists tightened. "I'm sick of being teased." She lowered her chin and charged as she'd seen Boris do. Two-hundred pounds of angry girl smashed a jeering pigren to the ground, and she trampled it into the mud with her one shoe and one bare foot. The circle broke, and the squealing pigrens scattered. Renée bolted toward the sound of the flowing river. She was a good swimmer, and she knew pigs weren't. The trees thinned out, and the rocky ground bruised and lacerated her shoeless foot. A mixture of animalistic squeals and human chants of "Get her! Kill her!" whistled around her ears. Renée yelped as she felt the sudden poke of an occasional acorn strike the middle of her back.

The stony ridge dropped into the roaring currents of Savage River. Renée peered down at the foaming rapids far below. Sharp, angular rocks jutted from the water's sweeping surface. She'd have to run further down the ridge or, if she jumped in now, risk being sliced to ribbons. Renée spun around. The pigrens were gathered behind her, inching closer with their sharpened sticks. One jumped forward and speared her in the calf. She collapsed to the ground, moaning and clutching her leg. The pigrens jeered and snorted. "Leave me alone," she screamed, writhing helplessly on the ground.

A deformed hand reached out and seized her coat. Additional hands tore at her clothing. Renée shrieked and wrapped her arms around herself, clasping the pendulous, pale breasts that spilled out from her bra. As she squirmed, the pigrens poked at her with their wooden spears and kicked her wounded leg. "She looks like Mama," a palsied pigren with a drooping, yellow eye and a half-melted face giggled.

"Let's cook her!" another said, clutching his stick tightly and making jabbing motions at Renée.

"Roast the fat, little pig on a spit," another voice called from among the crowd.

Renée trembled, and her eyes darted from one menacing porcine face to another. Before she could scream, a horde of pigrens pounced on her and held her down. Her eyes widened as she caught sight of a silver blade, glinting brightly through the surrounding gloom. "Hurry up, I wanna cut her tits off," a pigren squealed, jumping up and down with glee.

Her head was forcibly held in place. Renee stared up into a pair of coal black eyes. The knife pierced the soft, flabby meat of her breast. A sickly fog swirled before her eyes, and Renee passed out.

***

Renée's eyelids fluttered open. Her arms and legs were heavy, and her chest hurt. She tried to move, but her wrists and ankles were bound with vines. Her feeble cries caught in her throat, and she broke into a violent fit of coughing. Silhouettes scurried close by, and she angled her head to look about her. The shifting shapes collected wood and were preparing a fire as well as any boy scout could. Waves of dizziness and pain rolled through her.

Two young pigrens sat beside her on a felled tree trunk. One used a piece of flint to fashion a long stick into a skewer. The other swung his legs and nonchalantly ate the sandwiches she'd taken from Donna. Smoke bloomed up behind them, and the air was fragrant with burning pine. Kindling crackled and spat, and flames leapt into the cold night sky. Renée's vision cleared, and she studied the two pigrens and their odd headdresses. Blood had dribbled from their faces and dried in dark rivulets on their chests like tribal tattoos.

Stones pierced through the cold, damp earth and dug into her back. Her limbs were numb from the tight vines. Renée panicked and thrashed her body from side to side. A blaze of pain burnt through her chest. She looked down. All that remained of her breasts were two bloodied gouges and a rim of yellow fat. Her face crumpled. Soft sobs of sorrow trembled from her lips. One of the pigrens on the log chuckled. Her eyes swivelled to him. The contents of her stomach erupted from her mouth. The odd hats the two pigrens wore were her breasts. Her body heaved again, and several pigrens raced over to sit on her.

A large, adolescent male with a pig's head, one human arm, and the other a tumorous, withered branch of skin stretched over bone grabbed the skewer and thrust it at her mouth. Renée clamped her jaws shut and shook her head vigorously. Her attacker grabbed her head and hammered at her lips with the stick, breaking her teeth into shards. Blood filled her nose and mouth, and she struggled to breathe. The pigrens cheered as the stick was shoved down her gullet, through her innards, and out her backside like a giant splinter. Renée convulsed in agony. The jeering faces swirled around her, and she slipped into the darkness once again.

Renée was jostled awake as the pigrens carried her over to the fire and set her onto two Y-shaped branches above the flickering flames. Scorching heat seared her back and her hair blazed. White-hot pain lanced through her body as she was rotated on the spit. The pigrens sang as she slowly turned:

"Upon our head we wear a tit

Of fat little pig roasting on a spit!

Chew her skin, chomp her meat

Fat little pig, so good to eat!"

Boiling blood spewed from her smashed mouth and hissed on the embers. Blisters bubbled on her charred skin; her buttocks cracked open. Globules of fat dripped and sizzled in the fire. The heady stench of slow-roasting pork violated her nostrils. The pigrens danced around the spit, whooping and singing, their strange, hungry eyes illuminated by the orange glow of firelight. Flames burst from Renée's flayed windpipe as she tried to scream. The pain drained from her. She glimpsed the faint light of stars peeping through the pink marshmallow clouds before her lashes burnt away and her desiccated eyeballs roiled in their sockets.

MINCED LEGS

The hook had pierced through the small of Janie's back and poked out from under her ribcage. Blood from the gash had slowed to a trickle, and although it hurt to breath, she was glad to be alive. The hook must have missed all her vital organs. She clung to the chain, hauled herself up slightly, and took some of the weight off the wound. She had never been more grateful to be a bulimic who weighed only ninety pounds.

Matt's wound was a pulp of jagged flesh. The pigman, with primal strength, had rammed the meat hook straight through his shoulder blade. The steel point had exited just below his collar bone, luckily missing the main arteries. Matt had drifted into unconsciousness. His chest gently rose and fell, and Janie could hear his shaky puffs of breath. The dead weight of his heavy body had torn the wound into a yawning mouth. Janie's makeshift tourniquet had been a lifesaver. The cleaver slash on his forearm was sealed with clotted blood.

Janie looked around the barn. Mama Dolores and her son no longer stood below her dangling feet. Marian watched her from afar. The sow's twitchy, watery eyes assessed her next meal. She didn't appear impressed at the lack of meat on Janie's bones, but whenever her eyes gazed at Matt, her fat, pustular tongue wormed over her lips, and drool dribbled from her mouth. Marian's pig-grub offspring wiggled on top of the mountain of naked, pink flesh and sucked noisily on her teats.

They needed to escape, and quickly. "Matt, wake up," Janie hissed. The boy didn't stir but hung limply on his hook. Janie swung toward him and grunted in agony as the hook wrenched at her flesh. "Matt, wake up. We need to get out of here." She stretched out her hand and tugged at his shirt.

Matt's eyes blinked open, and he stared blankly at her. "What's up?"

"We are." One side of his mouth curled in a slight smile. Janie saw, beneath the emo fringe and the multiple piercings, Matt was a hunk. His cool, ice blue eyes made her tingle. "Enjoying your latest piercing?" she asked.

"Not really. It's a bit too much, even for me."

"Matt, this fucked up family is going to kill and eat us. We need to get out of here somehow."

He looked down at the steel jutting out of his skin. "Yeah, how's that going to happen?"

"We've got to think of a way to get off these hooks." Tears spilled down Janie's cheeks. She didn't want to be cut up, boiled and made into a stew by these freaks. What the fuck were they anyway? When she was growing up in the city, she'd heard many wisecracks about how inbred and backward the country folk were. The kinds of jokes Americans made about the rednecks living in the deep south. But pig-human hybrids? This was taking fucked up to a

whole new level. How was it even possible to mate with a pig? There must be something in the water.

Mama Dolores strode into the barn. The pigman followed her. Garrett was slung across his back. "We gotta do some mincin'. There be a lotta mouths ta feed," she said. The red splotches on her face from the steaming mince were raised in blisters.

"Hurry up, Mama. We be hungry," Marian said.

"Nothin' beats fresh mince. It be just what a growin' family needs ta thrive."

The pigman dumped the semiconscious Garrett to the ground and tore at his clothes with his bare hands. Massive veins in his arms bulged as he ripped apart the heavy fabric. The old soldier was still in great shape, lean and muscular. Scars from bullet wounds puckered the skin of his chest and shrapnel marks peppered his chiselled abdomen and legs. Garrett's body was swollen with large purple bruises from where the pigman had beaten him. His buckled legs kicked out weakly, and a misshapen hand flailed at the pigman's face. The snarling brute grabbed Garret's arm, twisted it, and snapped it at the elbow.

"Garrett!" Janie shouted.

"Wh-wh-what the fuck is happening?" he said groggily.

"Ye goin' be minced," Mama Dolores interjected, putting the pails down beside a large object covered with a tarpaulin.

66

"We be hungry. Hurry, Mama, hurry," Marian said.

The pigman dragged Garrett by a limp arm to where Mama Dolores waited. She pulled back the canvas sheet to reveal an industrial-size mincer. Garrett tried to resist, but his legs scrabbled around like a spider on ice. His one free arm hung useless and broken at his side. Mama Dolores walked to the front of the machine and turned it on. The mincer rattled violently, and the rusty blades spun into a blur. "Feed 'im in," she said to her son.

"Oh god no. No, please, don't," Janie pleaded. Matt watched on silently as the pigman thumped his great hands onto Garrett's chest. The monster hoisted him up and dumped the man feet first onto the feeding tray. Garrett jerked his legs back. He stared in horror at the whirling machine inches from his toes.

"Feed the goddam city cunt in!" Mama Dolores barked, her thin, cracked lips pulled back over receded, black gums.

The pigman shoved Garrett along the tray. His feet disappeared, and his screams mingled with the sounds of crunching bone and squelching meat. He thrashed about wildly, but the pigman's grip was too strong. Pink mist sprayed into the air. Wet strips of flesh plopped into one of the pails as his calves were dragged into the mincer. Janie's stomach clenched. Hot bile gushed between her gritted teeth. Mama Dolores cut the motor. She peered into the bucket. "That be good, lean meat. Sogash goin' ta like that, that 'e will." In the silence, Janie heard the squeals of another pig outside the barn. Mama Dolores picked up the filthy bucket at her feet. "Sogash won't be wantin' ta wait once 'e 'ears ol' Betsy grindin' away."

"We be hungry, Mama," Marian hollered. The sow stomped her hooves against the straw. "We be hungry. Give us meat."

"Wait ye turn, girl. Be showin' some respect ta ye elders." Mama Dolores turned and smiled at Garrett. "And as for ye, don't ye be wanderin' off anywhere." She cackled and waddled from the barn carrying the bucket of shredded feet and lower legs.

The pigman stood and stared at Garrett who lay on the feeding tray, trembling. The old soldier was morgue white. His eyes were rolled back with shock, and his mouth gasped sporadically for air like a fish plucked out of the water. Spurts of blood pumped from his mangled stumps and flowed over the rim of the tray into the mouth of the mincer. Marian struggled to sit up. The piglets dropped from her; six bloated leeches engorged with their mother's milk. She sank onto her front haunches, crawled toward the pigman, and presented her gaping, fungoid cunt to him.

Her brother swaggered over to her and unzipped his overalls. His cock sprang out, beaded with pus and precum. He screwed it into his willing sister, and her greedy hole sucked in her sibling's cock like a vacuum cleaner. The pigman pounded Marian while the piglets squirmed around his boots, sniffing at the gusts of foul air their mother's flabby vagina farted out with each thrust.

"Garrett?"

His dull eyes swivelled to Janie. His head rolled drunkenly as he looked at where his legs once were. He fixed his gaze on Janie and eased his arm to the edge of the feeding tray. His fingers gripped the side, and he dragged his stumps from the mincer. Strings of flesh trailed from his severed legs as he launched himself from the tray and pitched to the floor. He lay there, twitching and struggling to breathe, before rolling onto his stomach.

The rutting, mutant pigs didn't notice Garrett inching in a caterpillar-like motion toward Janie. "Look at the blood, Matt. What's he doing?" Janie whispered.

"I think he's trying to reach the chain to let you down." The chain, anchored to a beam, was slung across the rafters. Janie sobbed as Garrett slid ever closer to her using his chin, fingers and stumps to move. His face was contorted in pain, and large pools of bright red blood streamed in his wake. The soldier in him and his stoic fortitude had come to the fore in his desperate, final moments of life.

The grunts from the copulating siblings reached a fever pitch. The piglets squirmed back under their mother and swung erratically from her swollen nipples. Garrett reached the post supporting the beam. The chain hung above him, and he would be forced onto his stumps to release them. "You can do it," Matt urged him on. "Don't give up."

The dying man craned his neck to look at the hanging boy. He nodded and forced his arm up the wooden post. Garrett curled his hand around it and hauled himself up. His stumps grated over the rough stones as he struggled for purchase. He stretched for the chain. His fingertips brushed the metal. Janie jerked her head toward the barn entrance. A bucket clanged against the disembowelled tractor, and Mama Dolores clomped through the gloom. "What ye doin'?" she snarled.

Her blood-stained hands dropped the bucket then wrapped around Garrett's clammy, bald head. She hauled him to the mincer and flung him back onto the feeding tray, his head now nearest to the blades. Janie wept for the courageous, old soldier and cursed the arrival of the old woman and her prodigious strength. The pigman detached himself from his sister. A long rope of spunk dangled from the tip of his cock and disappeared into the blackness of his sister's cavernous opening. "Makin' more young 'uns I see," Mama Dolores said.

"He filled me up good, Mama," Marian said. A dense, yogurt-like mixture oozed from her spasming hole.

"That be fine, but this 'un be tryin' ta get away while ye doin' it, idiot." Mama Dolores pointed to Garrett. Quick as lightning, she reached up and slapped the pigman across the snout. He let out a high-pitched squeal, and cowering into a corner, he rubbed at the bloody slime oozing from his nostrils. Mama Dolores stooped, ran her hand around the rim of Marian's slick cunt, and sucked her fingers. "Hmm. A good, salty load though, yessir. Good for fillin' up these 'ere woods with our kin."

"Can I have some meat now, Mama?" Marian pleaded.

"Fucking sickos," Matt muttered.

"This be 'ow we do things 'ere in Savage River," Mama Dolores said. "Always 'ave done."

"You're monsters," Janie cried.

"No, no, no, I told ye already, we be swine farmers. An' we be slaughterin' 'em for the meat. An' ye be the swine." Mama Dolores plunged her greasy finger, coated in jizz and cunt juice, deep into Garrett's eye socket. He groaned as she stirred her finger around in his skull. "Now, let's get this 'ere slab of meat minced for the morrow." Mama Dolores jabbed the start button on the front of the mincer. The blades churned, ready for the offering.

The pigman pushed Garrett by the stumps into the whirling steel. His head was thrust into the mincer. The skull cracked and splintered; hundreds of tiny bone shards spat from the machine. A tortured scream erupted from deep within Garrett's throat. His body convulsed. Brain matter dropped out the other side into the bucket. The pigman pulled Garrett from the whirring blades. The top part of his head was sheared off, his eyes, nose, ears, now all shredded to pink, indistinguishable sludge. Garrett's jaw twitched, and his tongue lolled over his lower teeth. Janie wailed in anguish. Matt turned his head away in disgust. The pigman dropped the cadaver onto the tray and guided the torso through, pulverizing lungs and ribs to meal. Viscera squirted from Garrett's ass, and the pigman scooped them up and tossed them back into the mincer.

Marian rocked from side to side and banged her trotters on the bucket as it slowly filled up. One of her piglets snuffled at the mushroom-like, purple fungi dangling from her hindquarters as if they were truffles. Mama Dolores finally turned off the machine. She smiled at the big pile of warm mince in front of her. Janie's sobs continued to sound above the squeal of delighted pigs and the slowly churning blades. The mincer flicked out the last pieces of Garrett then ground to a halt.

THE JOUSTING PIG DWARF

John curled into a ball. The pigman clomped along the aisle, snatching at bags, ripping them open, and scattering their contents. Whatever food he found, he crammed into his mouth. The snorting beast paused beside John's seat, grabbed his bag, and tore it open. His huge hand squashed the cream cheese and anchovy bagel into his mouth. It was John's favourite type of bagel, and he'd saved it for his dinner. *Please god, don't let me die. I promise to stop putting laxatives in Renée's Ovaltine, and I'll never call anyone a 'cunt' ever again.*

The crippled boy often wished he were dead. His life sucked ass. His permanent stiffy was a beacon to perverts, and his twisted pretzel of a body was a prison. Yet, at this very moment, when death loomed large over him and was eating his bagel, he realised he actually didn't want to die. Life wasn't bad ALL of the time. He loved his comic books and playing games on his PlayStation with the couple of mates he had back at Kimberly House - Lenny, the arsonist, who suffered from hydrocephalus, and Aafaaq, a gender-fluid midget with PTSD from having been forced to spend much of his early childhood living in a specially modified cage so he could sing like a canary to a wealthy widower. John also held onto the hope a drug would be developed in the future. A course of medication that would reverse the ravages of cerebral palsy so he could one day live out his dream of becoming a park ranger.

The sound of gagging then the splat of regurgitated food jolted John from his musings. The pigman spat out the last of John's bagel, roared, and wrenched John's seat from the railings. John curled up in a tighter ball, hugging his crippled legs against his pigeon chest. Glass shattered over him as the chair was flung through the window. The pigman continued his rampage along the aisle, manically ripping apart luggage. John couldn't believe the pigman hadn't seen him. *He must have been preoccupied by the search for food,* John thought. *The greedy fucker.* The beast kicked the scattered remains of their belongings along the aisle and tramped from the bus. John released his pent-up breath. He waited, cowering on the floor, and listened to the sound of the pigman's disgruntled grunts grow distant until they were swallowed up by the howling gale. The slanting rain lashed through the broken window, soaking his skin through the thin T-shirt. He shivered as much from terror as from the rain and the cold.

Life could be a barrel of steaming dog piss. In recent days he'd been paraded around and had to endure being nice to people at a fundraiser for a special off-road wheelchair. He was forced to have his photo taken for the local newspaper, smile at strangers after they dropped their donations into a bucket at his feet as if he were a beggar, and pretend not to notice their lascivious grins at his prominent boner. He'd been convinced to go on this camping trip to work on his anger issues, and the whole thing had blown up in his face. He'd been raped yet again, his counsellor murdered, and his life endangered. John wrapped his arms around himself and rocked from side to side, shivering and wallowing in self-pity. The soothing cry of a morepork gradually calmed his terror. *Get a grip, John. Life's shit, but at least you didn't end up like Donna.*

He crawled through the debris, scanning the mess for his coat. His mind explored the available options. He could stay on the bus and hope the pigman didn't come back. Maybe Garrett and the others would return with help. But what if the monster had gone off to hunt them down? What if they got hurt or were brutally killed as Donna was? He had to warn them. It was his only chance of getting out of this shithole alive. As much as he hated to admit it to himself, he needed the others. Safety in numbers after all. John guessed they'd still be trudging their muddy way to the farm, and there was a good chance they'd encounter the pigman out there in the dark. He needed to catch up to them, fast.

It was time to try out the Spaz5000 with its powerful 600W motor, four-wheel drive, and all-terrain tyres. Buoyed up with determination, John located an intact backpack and filled it with supplies: a first aid kit, a dry T-shirt, a bottle of water, a packet of Renée's squashed marshmallows the pigman had missed, and a torch. Garrett had taken the keys to the bus. The ramp wouldn't work without power. "How the fuck am I going to get this chair out of here? Fuck it, I'm going to drive this baby off the bus like that scene in *Speed*." He crawled onto the chair and strapped himself in.

"Let's do this," he growled. He turned on the headlamps and twisted the throttle to its maximum. The engine whirled to life, and the Spaz5000 shot forward into space. A slight bump and John flew out the doorway. He hurtled down the dirt road, his face prickled by rain, and congratulated himself on choosing the 'Mountain Man' additional shock absorber package. Donna's body wasn't sprawled out in the mud. The pigman must have dragged the cadaver off with him. John suspected there would be a roar from the woods when the pigman tasted Donna's anchovy bits.

The headlamps lit up the road and a narrow ribbon of the surrounding woods. John was grateful the lights didn't penetrate the trees. Ominous, inhuman sounds echoed from the gloom and turned his skin to goose flesh. The pigman was out there somewhere, stalking the others or, worse still, watching him as he rolled along the dark, winding track. He was too vulnerable. He needed a weapon. The beam illumined several branches lying on the side of the road before he spotted the contours of a stout branch. John manoeuvred the wheelchair alongside it, unbuckled his safety harness, and stretched to pick it up.

The limb was sturdy, over four feet long, but blunt. He flicked open the blade from his trusty 'Field Master' Swiss Army knife with fifteen functions and quickly whittled the end into a sharp point. It was only a sharpened stick, but it made John feel a lot safer. He was making good time too. The Spaz5000 moved like a monster truck across the rocks and bumps in the road. With the stick and the wheelchair, he felt like a real park ranger protecting Savage River from poachers and college students.

John continued onward; his eyes darted in all directions with each fleeting, disembodied sound coming from the trees. The rain eased to a drizzle, and the pelting drops no longer lashed at his wind-burnt skin. The glow of the headlamps shone on a smallish silhouette emerging from the darkness of the tree line. It stood statue-like in the middle of the road despite the oncoming vehicle. John slowed to a standstill and rubbed the spots of rain from his glasses. He heaved a sigh of relief when he saw the blurry figure was the height of a child, not a seven-foot monster. "Maybe it's the farmer's kid," John said. "Or a dwarf." John waved an arm in the air. "Help, help," he shouted.

The figure ran toward him. It had a stick too and shouted a few unintelligible words. As it drew closer, John didn't know if it was a trick of the light or his imagination, but the shape of the figure was all wrong. It resembled a miniature version of the pigman. The body was human, but the head porcine. Devoid of clothes, its exposed, wrinkly limbs and belly were rife with tumorous, pulsating growths. Brandishing its stick like a spear, the little, wizened monster charged at John, squealing angrily.

"Holy fuckhole!" John shouted. There was no time to spin the Spaz5000 around in retreat; the gap between them was shortening every second. He had to continue onward to warn the others. He had to fight. "Okay, you want some of John, do you, little guy? Well, come on then!" Sir John revved up his steed, lowered his lance, and charged. "Aarrrrgh," he bellowed. The majestic, mechanical animal, born of rubber and reinforced steel, vibrated beneath him. The wind tousled his hair as his noble stallion galloped straight at the miniature menace. John felt alive and exhilarated.

The pig dwarf suddenly threw his spear. With the reflexes of a crippled cat, John jerked his head to the left. The spear grazed his right cheek and slammed into the headrest. The pig dwarf leapt surprisingly high into the air. John braced himself and raised his lance. The sharpened tip pierced the pig dwarf's chest. Its body slipped down the length of the branch and crashed into John.

The wheelchair careened over the road, narrowly missing a ditch. John thumbed the emergency brake button while the pig dwarf's body pressed against him. Blood dribbled out the sides of the chest wound into John's mouth. He was suffocating under the cancerous pig flesh. John pushed the weight from him and recoiled as a torrent of blood gushed from the yawning mouth. The body thudded to the dank ground. John spat out the mouthful of blood and peered down at his attacker.

The head resembled a piglet with tiny pointed ears and a small, flat snout. Its creased, diseased body was hairless and immature. John cast his eyes over the undeveloped, tiny genitals. "Oh fuck, he's a child. I've killed a child." The pigboy's chest fluttered. His crooked, piggish fingers wandered weakly across the gape in his chest, and he squealed in agony. John reached for the first aid kit and rummaged through it, wondering what the hell he could use to treat a spear wound. He chose a pressure pad. John unfastened his harness and dragged himself down from his chair onto the cold, squelchy ground. The pigboy looked at him helplessly. Huge tears squeezed from his black eyes. "I'm going to help you okay, piggy?" John said.

A single pressure pad wasn't enough to stem the furious bleeding, so John placed his palm on top of it. The pigboy screamed as blood pumped from the hole, spumed from between John's fingers, and drenched them both. "Fucking hell, son, you're bleeding to death." He pressed down as hard as he could. The pigboy's eyes rolled back in their sockets. It was no use.

John stretched up and reached for the backpack. He shook out the contents, grabbed up the T-shirt, and rolled it into a ball. He'd seen kids being given CPR in the hospitals he'd stayed in, and once the wound was plugged, he positioned his hands over the heart and pushed. The T-shirt disappeared into the hole, followed by his hands. John yanked his arms back and stared in horror at his crimson fingers. John tried to roll the body nearer to the edge of the road, but the pigboy was too heavy and awkward for him. He wiped his bloody hands over his sodden clothes and looked down. "I'm so sorry, piggy. I'm so sorry. But you shouldn't have thrown a spear at my head, you silly cunt."

After John commando crawled back to the Spaz5000 and climbed onto his chair, he sped off down the road, leaving the dead pigboy in the dirt. He'd killed somebody. It wasn't anything like the Steven Seagal action movies he loved to watch. He could taste the coppery blood, feel the heavy body struggling, and wouldn't ever forget the life spark flickering out in his victim's frightened eyes. He hung his head in shame and wept. A wet branch slapped him in the face. The wheelchair had veered to the edge of the road. He needed to get his shit together. The others needed him more than ever. There was no telling how many of these vicious pig freaks were out here running about in the woods wielding spears.

The lights of the farmhouse appeared through the grey mizzle blanketing the horizon. John whooped in relief, and throwing caution to the wind, he accelerated to maximum speed and zoomed past the rusty, wire fenceline and overgrown fields until he reached the entrance. The gate had been left open and creaked in the wind. He sped through, ignoring the "TRESSPASSERS WILL BE" sign, and navigated his way up the steep hill towards the ramshackle house. Endless carcasses of farm machinery sprouting ugly weeds flanked the muddy driveway. "Ugh, typical," John moaned. The farmhouse didn't have a ramp for his wheelchair. He suspected country bumpkins took people with disabilities out back and shot them, so there just wasn't a need for any home adaptations. John slithered out of the Spaz5000 and used his elbows to climb up the porch steps. The front door was ajar, but he politely rapped on the flyscreen and waited.

KLO DAAX AG BODAR TOZ

Janie's head jerked up. The wound in her back throbbed, and the burning pain radiated through her chest and up her arms. A thin trickle of blood oozed from the gash below her ribs and dripped to the floor. To ease the pressure, she clasped the chain and pulled herself up. Dark spots swam before her eyes.

She must have passed out. When she came to, her arms hung limply by her sides, and the full weight of her body dangled from the meat hook. The wind whistled through the gaps in the roof and stirred the piles of straw beneath her. A strong smell wafted up, and Janie tilted her head to avoid the farmyard reek. Marian's snores reverberated through the darkness. The piglets were pressed up against her, fast asleep in folds of flesh. Outside the barn, the chirp of crickets and the croak of bullfrogs added to the cacophony.

Janie glanced over to the mincer. Old Betsy with her bloody maw and gore-splattered body looked like a dozing monster. Black smoke had billowed from the rusty steel grilles while the blades churned, and Janie hoped the old girl was in her death throes. She turned away. The screams, the squelching, the sight of Garrett emerging from the grinding plates as long, glistening, red worms haunted her. Janie covered her ears, and a look of anguished torment stretched over her face. He'd been so brave, and his last act was so selfless it broke her heart. Had they stuck to the main highway on their journey to the camp, he wouldn't now be pails of mince. "I keep seeing Garrett going through the mincer. I keep hearing his screams as he died. It was just so fucked up," she sobbed.

"Tell me about it. It was an agonising death," Matt croaked.

Janie looked across at her hanging mate. Matt's thousand-yard stare reminded her of a girl in hospital who'd witnessed her mother being flattened by a crane while she waited to pick her up from school. "If we get out of this, we'll need Donna to counsel us for the rest of our lives."

"As if we didn't need to be anyway." Matt grimaced. He was deathly pale, his eyes sunken into their sockets. A puddle of congealed blood darkened the floor beneath him. He didn't bother trying to take the weight off his own wound. His body hung limply like a marionette, swaying gently from side to side. Matt peered around the murky barn, and his eyes rested on the chain holding them up. "Do you reckon you could reach the end of that chain if I give you a push?" he asked.

The chain was several feet away. Janie doubted she could reach it, but she'd give it a good try. There was no other option except to hang around waiting to be fed into old Betsy. She clasped the chain holding her up and swung her legs and hips. On the third attempt, she gained enough momentum to reach Matt. He was waiting for her and gave her a push which sent him in the opposite direction. They repeated the manoeuvre like some macabre circus act. Janie could get no closer than a foot from the end of the chain, no matter how high she sailed or how far she stretched out her arms.

"It's no good, we'll have to think of something else," Matt said. Janie gradually rocked to a stop. The pendular movement had really hurt. Her lips trembled from the pains stabbing through her back like hot poker irons. She clamped her teeth over her lower lip and blinked away the tears. She didn't want Matt to think she'd lost all hope. The hook had wedged itself in deeper; the trickle of blood transformed into a steady stream.

They hung in the gloom waiting to be slaughtered. There would be no waking from this shared nightmare. Janie needed to distract herself from their impending fate. "Do you mind if I ask you a personal question?" she asked.

"Shoot."

"What's with all the devil tattoos? Do you worship Satan or something?"

"Just a rebellious phase I was going through."

"And the cutting?" She'd met dozens of self-harmers in hospital. Usually teenage girls with personality disorders or attention seekers. Some professed to having suffered personal trauma - their uncle finger banged them when he came over to babysit, they'd been date raped on a night out, their parents had stopped their pocket money, telling them it was time to get a job. Matt didn't look like the type of guy that would have been fingered.

"Same phase." Matt turned his head and gazed out of the barn window. The glass was clogged with dirt and dust, but through the layer of grime, a few stars shone among the black tendrils of the tree canopies. Janie thought that was the end of the discussion. She glanced over at the sleeping sow. A thread of drool dangled from her slack jaw and hung suspended above the head of a twitching piglet lost in a dream. She imagined feeding Marian and her devil spawn into the mincer. She imagined throwing Mama Dolores and the pigman in afterward and listening to the squeals of distressed pigs followed by the agonised screams of Dolores and her son flooding her ears. Matt interrupted her ghoulish reverie.

"When I was thirteen, I came home from school with a black eye after a fight in the playground. I'd been bullied my whole life, you see. Mr Vesper, a neighbour in our block of flats, found me crying on the doorstep. He said if I wasn't man enough to win my own fights, he had something special for me in his flat.

I was suspicious, of course. For all I knew he could have been a kiddie fiddler, and this was a ruse to get me alone in his flat. After years of bullying, though, I was desperate and went along with it. Besides, he might give me a gun, a pair of nunchakus, or something else really cool.

Mr Vesper's flat was a shithole, like the farmhouse. He was a hoarder and rarely went out. Each room was cluttered from floor to ceiling with junk. It stank too from stale tobacco, sulfur and cat shit; though, I never actually saw any cats in his flat. Poor creatures were probably buried alive under all the filth. And the sulfur, I couldn't compute why an old man's home smelled of it unless he'd been eating too many eggs, which is possible I suppose.

As I was about to make a hasty retreat, Mr Vesper plonked a mouldering tome in my hands. He said he was going into a nursing home and wouldn't need it anymore. *Klo Daax Ag Bodar Toz.*"

Janie furrowed her brow and pursed her lips.

"That was the book's title. It translates roughly to 'The Book of Demon Summoning.' Mr Vesper said it was a grimoire from the old country. The cover was made from the flayed skin of a witch and the pages from the fibres of a hanging bough. He said I could use it to perform dark magic on my enemies. Well, that night I attempted to summon a demon. It called for a blood sacrifice so I cut myself. That was the first time I self-harmed, so to speak."

Matt held up his left palm. An ugly, purple scar ran from his thumb to his pinky.

"Did a demon come?" Janie's eyes were wide, eager for the answer.

"The demon came alright. A fire imp called Szat. He was half my height and twice as wide, but light as air. And his eyes glowed as red as the lakes of hell. Two ivory horns stuck out of his head. He looked a bit like a giant toad the way he squatted and hopped about. Anyway, I sent him to get revenge on the kid who'd given me the black eye.

Szat woke me in the early hours of the morning, said the kid was toast, and promptly vanished back from whence he came in a puff of sulfuric smoke. I didn't believe the kid, Tommy Bunting was his name, had been taken out until the headmaster announced his death the next morning in assembly. I couldn't help it, but I didn't feel anything but glee at the news. I was happy Tommy was dead, and I had to try my hardest not to burst out laughing right then and there."

"That's... incredible," Janie said. Matt shook his head solemnly.

"After Tommy died, I got a taste for revenge. I became addicted to meting out vigilante justice. Anyone who'd pissed me off in my past was instantly incinerated. Of course, I had to carve myself up for each summoning, but it was a small price to pay. I got into the whole satanic thing in a big way. I covered myself in devil tattoos, listened to Norwegian black metal, and professed to being the son of Lucifer.

I was doing my father's work, and no one suspected me. It was easy. On the television news, the perpetrator was identified as a deformed, chubby dwarf wearing a devil costume. They called him the Barbecue Killer."

"Wait, what? I heard about him. They called it, 'The Summer of BBQ.' People walked around the city streets carrying fire extinguishers. City officials and celebrities went as far as having firemen as bodyguards. Everyone was paranoid they'd be torched next," Janie said.

"Yep, that was me. I chalked up over thirty victims and looked like a walking advertisement for a bad razor company. My parents noticed all my scars and cuts and insisted I get help. They thought I was depressed. We had a big fight about it. I lost my temper and had Szat burn down the house with them and my kid sister inside. When I cooled off, I realised what I'd done and was racked with guilt. I turned myself in and confessed to everything. The authorities thought I was suffering post-traumatic stress and didn't believe a word. Instead of jail, they sent me to the nut house."

"So, you really killed your parents and sister?"

"Yeah. I did that, though, not Szat. The demon was a psychosomatic symptom of my illness, a 'visual hallucination' the doctors said. You wanna know something really fucked up? I kind of miss him. Szat was funny as fuck and my best friend. My only friend. Pathetic, huh?"

Janie was inclined to believe the doctors too. Matt was a messed-up kid who obviously harboured a lot of guilt for what he'd done, and yet after everything they'd seen so far at Savage River, summoning a demon suddenly didn't seem all that preposterous. "I'm your friend, Matt. We're in this shit together. 'Til the end."

"Thanks." Matt managed a fleeting smile. He looked as if he were about to tear up. "Mind if I ask you something now?"

Janie averted her eyes. She didn't like talking about herself. Her past wasn't as screwed up as Matt's, but it certainly wasn't anywhere near normal.

Matt waited for a minute for her to reply and when she didn't, he added, "It's just I saw your surname on a list of people coming on the trip, and it was Japanese. You don't look Japanese."

"My parents are Japanese. I'm adopted."

"Oh wow, that's so cool."

"It isn't," Janie snapped, sounding harsher than she meant to. "They have certain expectations of me and let's just say, I don't meet them."

"Like academic?"

"No." Janie gazed down at her feet. She didn't want to talk about it anymore and Matt took the hint.

The awkward silence between them, interspersed by Marian's loud snores, was broken by the sound of shuffling shoes scuffing over stones and treading through straw.

PANCAKES

John rapped on the flyscreen again. He waited, but no one answered. If Garrett and the others were here, they should have heard him by now. Fat droplets of rain dripped through the porch roof onto John's head and slid down his neck. He pressed himself against the door and strained to listen. The house was silent. He had the right farm; he was certain of that. It had been the only one for miles. He hitched open the flyscreen. The stench of warm, fetid rubbish rushed out to greet him through the gap in the doorway.

"Hello?" John said, opening the front door. "Hello? Is anyone in?" A light from a single bulb flickered overhead. It cast long shadows across a corridor strewn with piles of filth. John used one hand to cover his nose and mouth. Despite the foulness of the house's interior, he had to go inside and see whether the others were here.

He couldn't crawl through the rubbish; he had to walk. *Come on, John,* he thought, *get those legs working and those feet moving.* John gripped the door frame to lift himself up. His legs flopped about as if they were made of rubber, but he managed to achieve a modicum of balance when he leant against the wooden jamb. John looked down at the fragments of a broken mirror that reflected back his anxious expression. *That's it, that's it, good. Now slowly let your legs take your weight. Easy does it. Don't rush. Take baby steps just like the physiotherapist said.*

He edged forward cautiously. John knew he could do it. Mummy was wrong. He tried to tell her time and time again that when he really put his mind to it, he could walk, sort of. She wouldn't listen, though. "Stay in your chair, Johnny boy, don't try and be normal. Mummy will look after you," she insisted. "There's no shame in having special needs these days. In fact, you'll be treated like a king. A crippled king. People will feed you, dress you, and wait on you hand and foot for your whole life. They'll bathe you too. Now, come on, let me wash your big willy before Daddy comes home from work."

John turned as the door slammed, shutting out the spiteful wind and his painful memories. Drafts of air continued to rattle the decrepit farmhouse's creaky joints. John swallowed as he shuffled further into the hallway, using the wall for support. It was coated in black grime, and his fingers brushed against soggy, peeling, floral wallpaper. His uncoordinated, inverted feet moved through the debris and pushed a path through the garbage.

He paused at the first open doorway and peered in - a sitting room cluttered with dusty furniture draped in tatty, frayed sheets. An ancient AWA television with its small screen boxed in by panels of wood, which made it look more like a sideboard than an electrical appliance, sat in the middle of the room surrounded by stacks of yellowed newspapers and empty tins. John lurched back as his eyes locked onto a human shape in the corner. The shape didn't move. John let out a sigh of relief when his eyes adjusted to the darkness, and he found himself staring at a faceless mannequin half hidden in the gloom. Broken tricycles encircled the plastic figure.

Shambling past more doors, John followed the smell of cooked food to the end of the corridor. In the dining room, three bowls of stew were left untouched on the table. John staggered toward them, licking his lips. His finger poked at the meat floating around in a greasy, watery broth. It was cold. Even though he was famished, the slop in front of him wasn't the least bit appealing. He surmised whoever the food was for didn't like it either. The stew pot lay empty and upturned by John's feet. Congealed lumps of meat were splattered over the table and the floor. Chairs had been pushed over. No doubt the dinner guests were in a hurry to rush outside and be sick. John raised his eyebrows as he noticed Matt's black backpack, covered in heavy metal patches, by one of the chairs.

John wobbled toward another door, holding the dining table whenever he felt himself about to drop. He pushed it open timorously. "Matt? You in here?" he hissed. The door led through to a rustic kitchen with a wood fire stove. It was messier than when Renée made her pancakes at Kimberly House. The foul smell of spoiled, raw meat permeated the air. John's stomach churned at the sight of grubs and beetles crawling over the dirty plates, and he turned away from the sink. The colour drained from his face, and he froze with horror. A foetus lay buried in its own eviscerated guts in a mixing bowl on the countertop. A long, thin umbilical cord was still attached to its torn belly and coiled around the little neck. The placenta, looking like a flattened jellyfish, hung over the rim of the bowl.

"What the fuck?" John gulped. Had he walked into a backwoods abortion clinic? Had some knocked-up girl, used as the family Fleshlight, given herself an abortion with the meat fork? The tiny corpse gave off a sweet, rotten aroma. Uninvited bile surged up his throat, and he retched trying to expel the horror. If Garrett and the others had stumbled on an illegal abortion clinic, then his fellow campers would be in serious trouble. They could be held somewhere in the house or worse. There was no way Renée could handle being a prisoner, especially out here in the country. John had forced her to watch *Deliverance* before they packed to go camping. Even though Renée was greedy and stupid, John had a soft spot for the girl. They had a common bond. Society shunned them for being physically handicapped. They were both victims of physical and mental abuse. Life pissed on them from a great height, but somehow she still had the tenacity to pick herself up and carry on with a smile. She had the resolve to keep on making fucking pancakes.

He needed to help them, and he needed protection for himself. He rifled through the drawers, disturbing a large family of cockroaches, until he found a butcher's knife. John shuffled back into the corridor. A newfound courage and purpose bubbled up inside him, and he puffed out his chest. John had a proper weapon now and felt ready to take on another pig child should the instance arise, but he mumbled a quiet prayer hoping that he wouldn't encounter the fucking steroidal monstrosity who had killed Donna.

John entered another room off the corridor. It was crammed with open boxes spilling out a jumbled assortment of mouldy clothes and shoes of different sizes. A large double bed was smeared with what looked like and smelled like pig shit. Dried fly husks littered the grimy windowsills, and green mildew stained the walls. John backed away from the overwhelming stench and shut the door. The adjacent door led down to the basement. John pulled a tattered string to turn on the bulb. A dull light illumined the stone steps and the handrail twisting into the murkiness below.

Moving through the house without a wheelchair or crutches was one thing, but stairs were another. John simply didn't have the strength in his legs, but Garrett and his camp mates might be held captive down there. He had to investigate, even if it meant he had to do so on his hands and knees. John crawled down backward, the butcher's knife clasped in his hand. His boner bunted against each step. When he wrestled his legs over the last riser, his body was so exhausted he rolled over onto the damp concrete and lay there, eyes closed and breathing heavily. His ribs felt bruised, and his nostrils were clogged with dust.

The realisation the others likely needed his help forced John up into a sitting position. He peered around in the semidarkness and dragged himself across the cold ground to the nearest stone wall. The basement was less cluttered than the house, and plumes of dust puffed up around him. He used the wall to haul himself up to a standing position and rested against the smooth stone. A children's horse rocker with a motley mane, a tattered couch, and an old, doorless wardrobe overflowing with moth-eaten clothes emerged from the gloom. John scanned the furry, grey mounds scattered over the floor. Decaying rats, their putrefying remains clinging to their skeletons, lay in puddles of grease on the concrete. Big spiders sat among the ceiling beams in webs heavy with dead insects and smaller spiders. A large book of nursery rhymes lay on the stained couch, its worn cushions bulging over the busted springs. The pages had been creased open to the story of 'The Three Little Pigs'. John was sick of fucking pigs. He snatched up the book and hurled it against the wall.

At the end of the basement was an iron door similar to those on ships. John pressed his ear to the cold metal and held his breath. A peculiar, erratic wheezing came from the other side. It sounded a bit like Renée. *Is it really her?* John wondered. *Could she have been imprisoned by that hideous pig fuck who murdered Donna?* John knew a little of Renée's history. Surely that wasn't happening to her again? His mind juggled with his thoughts as he wrestled with the sliding bolt latch. The door was heavy and took all his strength, but spurred on by the prospect of finding Renée, he managed to open it. The room was pitch black, and no joyful Renée ran from its depths to wrap herself around him. The air was saturated with a ripe, rancid smell that coiled around him. "Renée?" he whispered. A huge bulk stirred in the depths, and the ground vibrated beneath his feet. John could hear a chorus of geriatric wheezing, and his cheeks tingled from the blasts of hot air fanning over his face.

John slammed the door shut and fumbled the bolt across. His legs folded under him and he slid to the floor. Something hefty pounded against the door. John rubbed the back of his head where it had collided with the concrete. His probing fingers found a large, tender spot but no blood. He dragged himself to his feet. Some fucked up shit was going on in this house, and he didn't want to stick around. He could only hope Garrett and the others hadn't already been introduced to whatever lay in the basement. After an exhausting climb on his hands and knees back up the steps, he staggered through the house and made his way to his wheelchair parked by the porch. If the others were still alive, they were being held against their will elsewhere. From atop the hill, John noticed the slanted roof of an outbuilding protruding above the treetops. *A barn*, he thought. *Maybe they're in there.*

FOOD FOR OL' SOGASH

"Time ta get mincin'," Mama Dolores said clapping her hands.

Janie grimaced. The flesh around the embedded meat hook was hot and swollen. The pain burnt down her back and across her shoulders.

"We be hungry, Mama," Marian whined sleepily from over on her straw bed. She dragged herself to Mama Dolores, the deformed piglets still latched onto her teats.

"Stop ye hollerin'." Mama Dolores kicked Marian in her soft flank, making her squeal. "Ye'll be fed later." Mama Dolores wore the same filthy apron stained with grease and Garrett's blood, but her faded, yellow sundress had been exchanged for a white one with a floral pattern. The pigman lumbered behind his mother, a large pail in each hand. His bulk formed a menacing shadow across the barn. "Undress 'im," Mama Dolores said, pointing a stubby finger at a drowsy Matt.

Matt's legs scrabbled at the air as if he were trying to run away. The colour was drained from his face. A fine sheen of sweat glistened on his waxen skin. Fresh blood from Matt's shoulder wound soaked his clothes, and the gash in his forearm looked scabby and inflamed. His ice blue eyes had lost their sparkle. Sunken in their orbital sockets, they stared dully ahead as the pigman approached.

The pigman grasped Matt's jacket and tore it off in one jerk. He did the same to Matt's underclothes and jeans and left them in a sodden heap on the ground. Matt's lily-white flesh was mapped with scars. Demonic tattoos and satanic symbols were doodled all over his skin. A large, black and grey depiction of Baphomet was etched on his belly. Pentagrams were tattooed on his pecs, a pierced nipple at the centre of each five-pointed star.

Janie counted more scars than the number of victims Matt had confessed to. Her mind raced. She desperately wanted this nightmare to end. "Why are you doing this to us?" she cried. "We've done nothing to you. We were just going camping for the weekend!"

Mama Dolores stared up at the whimpering girl. "Times be 'ard in Savage River. Not much swine ta farm. 'Ave ta take what we can get. Family need ta eat. Need ta stay strong an' breed so we don't done die out."

"But this is murder," Janie sobbed. Maybe she could buy Matt some time, convince this woman to back off, or scare her enough to delay the mincing until help came. "You won't get away with this. People will search for us."

Mama Dolores smirked. "I be 'oping so, more food for us, an' more food for ol' Sogash." She glared at Matt's feet. "Take off them there socks, ye imbecile. No one be eatin'" Matt kicked his feet and tried to make it difficult, but the pigman grabbed both of his legs with one massive hand.

With the other, he yanked off Matt's socks and flung them to the ground.

"Who's Sogash?" Janie asked.

"A god. Stupid girl. Don't ye know anythin'? Sogash be 'ungry after gettin' a taste of that there mature swine ye be callin' Garrett, an' 'e be wantin' more. Can't ye 'ear 'is 'ollerin'? Listen up."

Janie cocked her head to the side. She could hear distant, sweeping grunts echo through the woods that she'd presumed was the roar of the wind.

"We be hungry too, Mama," Marian said, looking up hopefully at her mother. She tugged on Mama Dolores' grotty apron.

"Ye be shuttin' ye mouth, girl. I be givin' ye what ye be gettin' when I be ready. Tend ta ye babies."

"These things," Janie gestured to Marian with a flick of her head, "are they his spawn?"

"That thin' be me babe, and this 'ere big 'un be one an' all. Now, best we not keep Sogash waitin' any longer. 'e 'as a power over these 'ere woods. Can control the weather an' such like. When 'e's 'ungry or when 'e's mad, 'e 'as a tendency ta cause all sorts of trouble."

"But…"

Mama Dolores put her finger to her lips and said "Shhhh. It be mincin' time."

"Mincin' time, mincin' time." Marian drummed her hooves on the barn floor beside the heads of her nuzzling pig grubs. She drooled uncontrollably. Her maggot-like body undulated as if it were full of fluid.

"I never believed what the doctors said, Janie," Matt hissed under his breath. I knew Szat was real. The book's in my bag at the farmhouse. If you could get to it, then you'd be able to…" His voice lifted several octaves to a scream as the pigman seized him around the ankles and pulled. There was a crack like a tree splitting in half, and Matt was torn free from the meat hook. His arm remained dangling on the steel spike. Matt's scream faded as he passed out. His shoulder spurted jets of blood across the straw-strewn ground. The pigman slung Matt over his shoulder, unhooked the arm, and dumped him in the mincer tray, head first.

Janie begged Mama Dolores to reconsider what she was doing to the poor boy, but the matriarch was not to be distracted and ignored her. Janie could do nothing to help Matt. She needed more time. If what he said about Szat was true, the book wouldn't do them a scrap of good back at the farmhouse. Mama Dolores punched the start button on the mincer. Janie prayed it wouldn't start, but old Betsy rattled, spluttered, and the gore-splattered blades whirred to life inches from Matt's head.

"Feed 'im in nice and slow. Sogash likes ta taste the fear," Mama Dolores said coldly. Her son acknowledged the instruction with a loud snort. Mama Dolores slapped Matt across the face. His eyes flicked open. "Wake up, swine. I want ta see ye face as ye be minced." She cackled. The pigman grunted and held Matt's remaining arm to the mincer. His fingers were sucked in. The flesh ripped from his hand. Finger bones crunched. The meat plopped out the other side into the pail. Slowly, the pigman fed the limb through the blades until he reached the shoulder. Janie screamed for Matt as he passed out again. Mama Dolores grabbed his hair and whipped Matt's head back and forth until he regained consciousness. "Wake up, city cunt! Wake up, swine!"

Janie trembled, wailed, hugged herself. Garrett's agony flooded back to her, and she was now witnessing Matt's torture. Despair overwhelmed her, and howls of grief shook her thin body. "I'm sorry, Matt," she cried. " Oh god, I'm sorry."

"Do his feet next, Mama," Marian said. A pig grub sputtered a mouthful of milk onto its overzealous mother. Mama Dolores nodded. The pigman dug his blackened fingernails into Matt's scarred flesh, spun him around, and shoved his twitching feet into the mincer.

Old Betsy vibrated and smoked. The machine worked hard to chew up the boy. Ground meat and grated bone spewed into the pail. The pigman pushed Matt forward along the tray. Matt glimpsed the grisly sight of his legs disappearing into the blades and flopped back. The pigman grabbed him up and shook him roughly until Matt responded.

A gleam returned to Matt's bloodshot eyes. A deep rumble swelled from his chest. "Hail Satan, Ruler of the Netherworld, Master of the Ninth Circle of Hell, Beneath the Celestial Prison of Descent....," Matt said. The pigman pushed Matt's pelvis into the mincer, splattering his own porcine face with blood. "...This life has ended but the journey has only just begun. I ask you, Father, to guide me to the next stage of existence. May my soul forever retain the wickedness and avarice it once knew." The mincer crunched through hips and groin and sucked up soft organs and liquid-filled tubes. Matt spat blood from his mouth. Pink mince flecked with white bone spilled over the rim of the pail. Mama Dolores carted it away and replaced it with the empty one. "Agios O Satanas, Agios O Satanas, Agios O Satanas."

Matt repeated the mantra over and over until his lungs were shredded. Janie looked away as his torso was pulverised to mush. When she returned her stare, all that was left of Matt were two heaped pails of wet, steaming meat. Mama Dolores plunged her hand into the warm mess. She rubbed a lump of mince between her fingers. "This meat be good an' tender." She lowered her face ta the mound in her palm. "Be smellin' good an' rich. Sogash gonna be pleased." She let the mince flop from her fingers back into the pail, ignoring Marian who snuffled at her legs. "Now, let's be takin' our offerin' ta 'im."

The pigman picked up the two pails and followed Mama Dolores out of the barn. Janie watched as they trundled away, Matt's remains sloshing over the sides. She listened to Sogash's grunts grow more frantic. The god's distant calls carried on the wind and chilled Janie to the marrow. "We be hungry," Marian sobbed. Her brood snorted around the mincer, looking for spilled morsels. "We be so hungry, Mama."

HOG ROAST

"Have some of this, you mutant hog bitch." John waddled out of the shadows wielding a scythe above his head. His withered legs were splayed and his mighty cock erect. Janie peered through the strands of damp hair clinging to her face and gasped. John was the last person she expected to see. She thought he'd have been long dead by now. His beetroot red face was twisted in rage, and his bug eyes were magnified by the lenses of his glasses. He wobbled toward the sow, undaunted.

Marian stared back at him like a deer caught in headlights. "Mama, Mama," she wailed.

"Die, pig whore. Die, die, die." John lurched forward. The scene played in slow motion. Marian's offspring stopped their feeding and gaped at him.

"Kill her," Janie screamed. She hated this fucked up family. They were murderous psychopaths, every one of them. Dumb, whingeing, whining Marian deserved to die. The gluttonous, ugly sow was a cruel, blood thirsty mutant, monster.

Marian squirmed backward and slumped against the barn wall. Her chubby legs kicked the air. She squealed hysterically. John brought the scythe down. The momentum made him stumble forward and fall on his knees. Marian's gut was slashed open. Coils of rubbery intestines erupted from her split belly. A dozen squirming foetuses clad in their translucent sacs splashed to the ground. The slimy, wriggling embryos were a mixture of animal and human parts. Piggish bodies were topped by humanoid heads. Porcine faces clashed with newborn baby torsos. Nascent limbs were no more than rounded, pink nubs that looked like little thumbs.

John scrambled back to avoid the flowing viscera. A puddle of blood grew steadily beneath Marian, and her nose twitched at the aroma of the steaming offal hanging out of her. She licked her lips. Struggling onto her haunches, she stood precariously over the hot mess. More of her slick innards splatted onto the floor. Her face lowered slowly to the mound of meat. She started to gorge herself on the grotesque banquet. "Ewww, the nasty fucker," John said, looking away. He put a hand to his mouth as he heaved.

"She's... she's... eating herself," Janie said, trying to fathom what she was seeing. No sooner had Marian scoffed a mouthful of chitterlings than the masticated dollop fell out of the gaping hole in her belly. Foetuses and piglets splashed and slithered in the deep pool of blood spreading around her.

John crawled over the straw and stones until he reached the chain used to keep Janie's meat hook suspended in the air. He clutched a wooden beam and stood up. "I'm going to let you down now, Janie."

"Okay. Do it slowly. It hurts so fucking much." She braced herself for a rough landing. John unhooked the chain. Her weight jerked his puny body upward, and Janie dropped to the ground. Her legs buckled, and she collapsed moaning.

"Shit, sorry about that. I wasn't strong enough." John crawled over to her. "Are you alright?"

Janie looked down at the hook protruding from under her ribs. The fall had caused the gash to bleed again. Thick, yellowish pus mingled with the dark, crusty blood, and angry, red streaks radiated from the wound. Sweat beaded her forehead. "No, I'll never be alright after this." She fought back tears at the thought of returning to hospital. Only this time, it wouldn't just be for an eating disorder. She now had the added trauma of having been terrorized by cannibalistic, mutant pig people. How the fuck could she ever live a normal life again?

"I wanted to save Matt. I saw what happened to him through a hole in the wall, but I knew I couldn't do anything to help. That… that pigman… I saw him kill Donna. I wouldn't have been able to stop him from doing what he did to Matt." John's eyes were swirling pools of misery.

"Donna's dead?" Janie whimpered.

"Uh-huh. I hated her, but the way she died was so fucked up." John's jaw trembled. Janie wondered how the poor kid would cope with the nightmare they shared.

"It's okay, John, you did the right thing. You were very brave to stay." Janie struggled onto her knees. A look of agony stretched across her face.

"Should we take out the hook?" John asked.

"No, I don't think so. It would make it bleed too much." Janie staggered to her feet and swayed unsteadily, waiting for the dizziness to pass. "Did you come by yourself, or is there help on the way?"

"I'm alone." John took hold of Janie's arms. "I had to come and look for you guys to warn you about the pigman. Guess I was too late." The two of them rocked back and forth, struggling to stand.

"So, no one knows we're here then," Janie said.

John sighed. "Did Renée get minced too?" He studied Janie's face. From the desperation etched on his own countenance, she could tell he cared for the girl.

"She ran away when she saw a pig at the farmhouse," Janie said. Marian belched and continued to scoff her own entrails.

"That sounds like her. She hates pigs." John's shoulders relaxed. "I hope she's safe."

"Me too."

"Knowing Renée, she probably ran straight into a tree and knocked herself out. What about Garrett?" John asked.

Janie shook her head despondently. "He got minced." Garrett's mangled body crawling at her feet flashed in her mind, and his screams echoed in her ears. She tried to block them out, but they wouldn't leave. "It was so horrible, John. I can't believe it happened. Garrett tried to save us, you know, even after his legs were gone." Violent sobs racked her body and made her ribs hurt even more, but she couldn't stop weeping. All the stress and horror poured out of her.

John patted her on the arm. "I know, man. This is some crazy shit. It's like a bad horror movie. I even killed a pig child on the way here." The slap of Marian's flesh as she toppled over, crushing her offspring, echoed through the barn. Janie sobbed for several minutes more. John waited patiently, though every so often his eyes darted around the dim interior, and his head cocked to the side listening for the return of the family. Janie straightened up and dashed her hand over the streams of tears. Like in a horror movie, if she wallowed uselessly in self-pity, she'd be a victim. They both would. She needed to be strong to get out of this macabre predicament alive, but more importantly, she needed to be strong if she wanted revenge.

Janie gritted her teeth and marched toward the piglets rooting around in their mother's blood. "It's fucking payback time." She seized one and dropped it onto the feeding tray. The piglet screwed up its hideous little face and cried. Janie flung more of the sow's spawn in next to it. Some tried to claw and scramble their way out. They knew exactly what the mincer was for. "We've got to make sure no one in this family survives. Otherwise, anyone else who ventures out here won't be safe. There's no telling how many people this messed up family have murdered and eaten."

She pressed the start button. Old Betsy rattled awake from her slumber. The piglets panicked. In an attempt to get away, they clambered over one another on the feeding tray. Janie punched one hard in the face, and it flew into the blades. Its minced remains were shat out onto the barn floor. John couldn't watch as Janie shoved the others into the whirling steel, and he slunk into the shadows.

Janie scooped up the foetuses from among the gore and excrement. A few still twitched. Janie thought of Garrett and Matt and threw them into the mincer. Not one of these inbred bastard monstrosities would be allowed to live. When the brood was no more than pink slurry, she turned off the machine. Black smoke drifted up to the support beams. "Matt said that he had a book in his backpack which can somehow summon demons. A fire imp. I want to get that book and cast a spell to light this whole fucking farm up." Janie wiped her hand on some straw.

"I know where the backpack is. I saw it at the farmhouse. It's by a chair in the dining room. But do you reckon it's true about being able to summon demons?"

"If you'd asked me that before this fucking camping trip, I would have said no, but now it's a definite yes. I do think it's all real. Ghosts, demons, leprechauns… hell, we've seen monsters with our own eyes so why wouldn't there be all sorts of supernatural shit out there in the world? What better way to avenge Matt, Garrett and Donna than by summoning a demon to torch these evil fuckers to kingdom come? And, if Renée didn't make it, let's torch them for her too."

John pounded his fists onto the ground. "Yeah, a fucking hog roast! That would be so badass. Let's do it. Let's go. Right now." He grinned. "You can hitch a ride on the back of my Spaz5000."

SZAT

Janie kicked at Marian's corpse. A thick cloud of flies rose from the open belly. Insects crawled over the sow's waxen face and buzzed excitedly in the swamp of masticated innards and minced piglets. Janie staggered around the bloated body and shuffled outside. She inhaled deeply and spat out the lingering stench of blood and excrement saturating the air in the barn. The brooding, iron grey sky of early morning reflected Janie's mood. Those sick bastards had tortured and murdered Garrett and Matt. The pigman had killed Donna too. They would all suffer and die.

John emerged from a bush, seated in his wheelchair. He drew up alongside her. "Climb aboard," he said, waving his hand in a grand flourish. Janie clambered onto the back.

The wheelchair sped over the field, churning up mud in its wake. Janie tapped John on the shoulder. "This is nice."

"It's the Spaz5000," John said proudly. "It's the best all-terrain electric wheelchair on the market."

Janie's heart raced. The meat hook jutting out of her side hurt like a son of a bitch. Jolting over the bumpy ground aggravated the gash, and bolts of pain shot down her arm to her fingertips. She clenched her teeth and hummed, determined not to spoil John's delight in the performance of his Spaz5000. John hid the wheelchair behind a tangle of bushes to the side of the farmhouse. Janie expected Mama Dolores or one of her mutant offspring to burst onto the porch and blast at them with a shotgun, but the house was as silent as a tomb. Janie crept up the porch steps.

Frail and exhausted, she clung onto John's arm. They took it in turns to check for any members of the pig family sneaking up behind them. Janie knew if the pigman found them before they retrieved Matt's book of demon summoning, she and John would be done for.

The door was unlocked. Janie nudged it open and peered through the crack. Mama Dolores's harsh singing voice echoed through the house. The sound came from the end of the corridor. Janie gripped John's arm more tightly. They tiptoed along the corridor, using the wall and each other for support. John edged along on his bendy, crippled legs as uncoordinated as a drunkard. Waves of dizziness washed over Janie. She struggled to focus as she glanced through the open doors off the hallway. The rooms were cluttered but empty of pig people.

They sidled into the dining room. The door to the kitchen was shut. "There it is," John mouthed, pointing to the backpack by the table.

"We need to kill that crazy, old hag first then we can concentrate on the book," Janie whispered. She snatched up a filthy knife from the table.

John paled at the news and gripped the back of a chair. Janie eased open the creaking door. She peeked through the gap, blocking her nose at the foul stench wafting through the opening. Mama Dolores had her back to them, and her arms were up to her elbows in a giant bowl of mince. Matt was being made into meatloaf. This was some twisted shit. The pig-fucking cannibal deserved to die. Janie motioned for John to pick up the meat cleaver lying atop a chopping board stained a crimson hue. He swallowed hard and lifted the heavy chopper from a pile of small bones and gristle. Together they crept forward, the crippled boy and the wounded girl locked arm in arm.

Sweat beads glistened on the back of Mama Dolores' neck, and the cushions of fat on the underside of her arms wobbled as she kneaded the bloody mince and sang:

"I'm ma mincin', mincin' all day long

I'm ma mincin', mincin' 'til the day's done

Gonna mince ye up 'til the work be through

Ye city cunts got what's comin' ta…"

Janie stabbed the knife in a downward arc, aiming for the patch of blotchy skin between Mama Dolores's shoulder blades. The blow was wild. Janie was too fraught. The knife grazed the back of the old woman's head, sheared along the side of her face, and sliced off her ear.

The severed appendage plopped on top of the mince. Mama Dolores screamed with pain. She slapped a meat-coated hand to the wound and wheeled around to face her attacker. Blood pumped through her fingers, spurted across the stacks of unwashed crockery, and splashed into the mixing bowl. Janie jabbed the blade at Mama Dolores's gurning face, splitting her lip and clinking against her foul teeth. The next blow sank into her potato-like nose and split it in two.

John stood in the doorway clutching the cleaver, his mouth agape. The frenzied woman grabbed the hook poking out of Janie's belly as the girl raised her knife to strike again. She rag-dolled Janie back and forth while the girl slashed wildly at Mama Dolores' arm. The blade cut through soft, billowy flesh.

Muscle tissue around the metal ripped, and the meat hook burst free. Janie clasped the gaping, bloody wound below her ribs and staggered backward. "Help, John, help."

Mama Dolores brandished the hook. The flesh of her arms swung in tattered, white ribbons. Her mouth was drawn back in a snarl and her eyes blazed with fury. "I'm ma goin' ta rip ye some more holes, girl."

John's jaw clenched. He lurched forward, hefted his skinny arm up high, and thudded the meat cleaver into the woman's chest. Mama Dolores grunted as the blade crunched into her ribs. The meat hook clattered to the floor. John yanked the cleaver out. A jet of blood spurted over him like a stream of red piss. He went berserk. Spittle flew from his lips, and the cleaver became a blur in his palsied hand. More blood and bits of flesh and bone splattered around him as he hacked into Mama Dolores. Her hand came off at the wrist as she tried to guard her face. She kneed John in the cock. A sound of cracking wood reverberated through the kitchen. John looked down. His once straight penis was now angled at forty-five degrees. Mama Dolores headbutted him in the nose and broke his glasses.

"Oww, you vicious cunt," he yelled as he reeled backward. Mama Dolores lumbered over to Janie and beat her with the bloodied stump of her arm. The wet appendage hammered against the girl's head as if it were a pestle. Janie slashed out with her knife. John, blind as a mole, jumped back into the fray and thudded the cleaver down again and again into Mama Dolores' snarling face. "You bitch! You whore! Fuck you, Mama, fuck you! I hate you! You and every other fucking slag cunt whore! Fuck you all! Fuck you all for touching me down there! It's not my fault my dick is always hard! Rapists! Pigs! Cunts! Arghhhhh! Twat!" Tears ran down his flushed face.

Mama Dolores' facial flesh hung from her skull in pink flaps. A blow cleaved into her neck, almost severing it. She teetered and toppled forward. Janie and John sprang out of the way. Mama Dolores hit the ground hard, making all the plates and pots rattle. As she lay face down on the floor, she made a gurgling sound like water disappearing down a plughole. Her limbs twitched momentarily as her life slipped away, and finally, she became still in the centre of a scarlet pool.

"You okay?" John asked, hobbling over to Janie's side. She'd slumped against the kitchen cupboards and held onto her belly.

"I think so. The bleeding is stopping. It just hurts a lot." She took a moment to rest. "Thanks for your help back there, John."

"No problem. Though, I think she broke my cock. Now, we need to get Matt's book before that big, ugly pig fucker sees we've hacked his mum up like a kebab. Man, I can't wait for this fun camping trip to be over."

They staggered through to the dining room. Janie retrieved Matt's backpack. Setting down the knife, she opened the zip. Her hands felt around inside, and she pulled out a toiletry bag, a drink bottle, and wrapped in a plaid shirt, a small book not much bigger than a pocket bible. "This is it," Janie said. "'Klo Daax Ag Bodar Toz', 'The Book of Demon Summoning.'" Matt wasn't lying. The grimoire was very old, the binding cracked and faded. Inside, the pages were yellow and spotted. Janie traced the lettering with her fingers. "I need somewhere quiet to read this."

"How about the basement? There's something down there locked behind an iron door. I reckon we should summon the meanest demonic fucker from hell and toast whatever it is next."

John, squinting, crawled down the stairs and led Janie to the dusty couch in the basement. Sogash sniffed and snuffled at the door, sensing someone was nearby. Janie gave the door a fearful glance before settling on the couch. John curled up beside her and craned his head to peer at the book. The grimoire was written in demonic speak, but Matt had painstakingly translated each word using Google Translate and rewritten the text on loose sheets of paper. Janie read from Matt's notes, just loud enough for John to hear:

"In the abyss, there are five types of demons: Dukes, Lords, Dark Knights, Squires and Squabs. Each demon requires various

sacrifices to be made before the summoning. The more powerful the demon, the greater the sacrifice. Dukes demand you to give your life."

Janie thought this request was a bit too steep so she read on:

"Lords want you to sacrifice a family member. Dark Knights ask for an organ. Squires are content with any appendage no matter how useful, and lastly, Squabs want a blood sacrifice (either your own or from a friend)."

The crude illustrations of the Dukes were terrifying. The Lords were no more personable. It was only when Janie got to the Squabs, she stopped shivering. They were a collection of runts. A podgy, baby-sized creature with a Kim Kardashian booty jumped out at her. "That's him," she said, pointing her finger at the sketch. "That's the type of demon Matt summoned to murder over thirty people."

"I can't see too well, but that demon doesn't look like much... Wait a minute, Matt murdered thirty people?"

Janie continued to read the text:

"Don't let his baby face fool you. Szat is a natural-born killer. Want your enemies painfully barbecued? Then you've summoned the right demon for the job."

Sogash snorted and clawed at the bolted door. "It says we need to make a fresh blood offering inside a pentagram for the spell to work," Janie added.

Janie used John's Swiss Army knife to scratch a five-pointed star onto the ground. She was about to cut her arm with the blade when John clasped her wrist. "It's okay, I'll do it. You've been through enough. I don't think you can risk losing any more blood." John took the knife from her. "Shame you're not on the rag, then we wouldn't need to do this at all." John cracked a smile. "Are you on the rag by any chance?" Janie shook her head. John sighed and cut into his forearm. He winced, then dripped the blood inside the pentagram. "Now what?" John said.

"We have to repeat these words to summon the demon," Janie replied.

"O kinnav dhoo ah rokkol

Konav dlan dho kadk ad horr

Dano vav uvk ka nav kakkavk."

They chanted the unfamiliar refrain. Their voices echoed off the brick and stone surrounding them. A red puddle suddenly appeared inside the pentagram, and a smell like burnt egg farts filled the room. The puddle began to smoke, solidify, and take form. Twisted limbs and an emaciated body that barely supported a pumpkin-sized head materialised in the centre of the star.

Janie and John gasped in unison. It had worked! They'd summoned a real demon. Unfortunately, the supernatural being didn't look at all like the illustration. It opened its lipless mouth and spoke. "Alright, which one of you cunts has cerebral palsy?"

GOING TO VALHALLA

"How was I supposed to know a demon took on the characteristics of its summoner?" John protested.

The demon glared at him. "It's on page one hundred and fourteen in black and white. Don't you read the footnotes?"

"No, sorry." John bowed his head.

The demon tutted. "Great. You're not mentally retarded as well as physically, are you? If you are, I'm proper fucked." The demon surveyed his crippled body and sighed. "I've had every kind of STD you can think of. I've had leprosy, a hump, a severe case of haemorrhoids, but never cerebral palsy. How the fuck am I meant to get up to naughty shenanigans looking like this?" He flexed his arms that looked like straps of beef jerky. "Name's Szat by the way." Szat took a step forward and face-planted on the ground. "For fuck's sake," he moaned.

Janie rushed forward to help Szat to his feet. His skin was hot to touch. She assisted the disgruntled demon to the couch where he sat with his arms crossed and his bottom lip pushed forward in a pout. "We need your help to burn down this farmhouse and kill the thing behind that door. A pig god." She pointed to Sogash's lair. "Some pretty fucked up shit is waiting for us outside too, like a hybrid pigman who gets off on mincing people," Janie explained, her face scrunched up from her throbbing wound. "Hard to believe I know."

Szat peered at the hole in Janie's torso. "Come here a sec, girlie. Let me finger you." The demon held up his index finger. The end of the digit was an amber cherry, glowing brightly. Janie shuffled back a step, unnerved by the offer. "I mean let me cauterize the wound. Geez." Before Janie could respond, Szat jabbed at the hole below her ribs. The flesh sizzled and smoked. She screeched then gagged at the meaty stench. "Now turn around so I can do you from behind. The other hole I mean." Szat's eyes darted to the iron door. "Wait a minute. Did you say 'pig god'?"

Janie nodded. Tears welled up in her eyes from the searing pain coursing through her, but the cauterization seemed to have done the trick. "Sogash or something," she mumbled.

"Duke Sogash, the Glutton of Prague?" Szat said. Janie and John shrugged. "Send me back now. I don't want any part of this." Szat slid off the couch. His legs buckled, and he face-planted on the floor again. "That guy is a right asshole. Mean as fuck even by hell's standards. Best to give him a wide berth if you know what's good for you."

"You can't go. We need you," Janie pleaded as she hauled Szat to his feet.

"I don't take orders from you, no-tits. I take orders from the retard."

"You're staying," John growled. "We need your help to make sure no other poor bastards ever stumble across this family again."

Szat looked around. "Where's Matt? The pale, angsty-looking fella who had me barbecue his family and half his schoolmates? I liked him."

Janie brushed away a tear. "He's… he's dead. This horrid family put him through a mincer. That's why we need your help. To get revenge."

Szat studied her for a moment. "Fine. But I want it down on record that I'm not happy about it."

"I think we should start the fire down here. That wooden wardrobe is full of old clothes and shit and once it catches alight the flames will spread quickly. Sogash won't be able to escape until the walls collapse, and he'll be crackling by then. My electric wheelchair's outside, and we can use it to make a getaway until we're safely back on the main road," John said.

"Ooh, check you out coming up with all the bright ideas, *Stephen Hawking*. Yeah, I'm crippled as fuck thanks to you. I'm not going trekking with legs like these. Pick me up and we'll get started." Janie scooped up Szat and put him on her shoulders. He was as light as air, just as Matt had told her. "Ready?" he said.

"Ready." Janie gave the thumbs up sign."

"Let's reduce this fucking shithole to ash." John grinned up at Janie and Szat. The demon held out his hands, palms toward the wardrobe. Heat radiated down the side of

Janie's face, and Szat's fingers glowed and crackled. Mini blasts of flame shot from his hands and exploded against the walls and furniture. Within seconds, the basement was an inferno. "You're going to have to hobble double time, *Forrest Gump*, if you want to get out of here alive. Chicks dig the size of my fireballs," Szat said to his summoner. "Nice cock by the way, but is it meant to be bent like that?"

Janie retreated to the stairs with Szat on her shoulders and John in tow. Smoke was curling along the corridor by the time they reached the main hallway. Below their feet, they heard Sogash grunting and slamming against the iron door. The stench of cooked meat wafted from the kitchen and out of the dining room doorway. They followed the aroma and were greeted by the sight of Mama Dolores bubbling on the kitchen floor, her flesh slow-roasting from the intense heat beneath where she lay. "I'm not even going to ask," Szat said. He melted the corpse with a jet of flame. The stench of charcoaled fat exploded into the air.

John tucked his nose into his shirt and tripped through the kitchen toward the back door. Szat flung fireballs around the cluttered room. The cupboards caught fire. The curtains blackened and burned. Janie and John groped their way to the door, and Szat, his hands acting as flamethrowers, set the entire kitchen ablaze. The heaps of garbage caught alight and spewed foul smoke. They stumbled from the burning house, coughing and gagging.

Szat, still seated on Janie's shoulders, murmured to himself as she breathed in the cool air. John dragged himself down the steps, and they headed over to where the Spaz5000 was hidden. Janie looked back at the smoke and flames billowing from the open windows. The roar of the fire resounded around her. Janie hugged herself. This was payback time for their minced and murdered mates. An immense feeling of satisfaction swept through her. Mama Dolores and her pig family had tried to take everything from her, and they hadn't succeeded. Instead, she'd turned the tables on them. Mama Dolores, her daughter Marian, and her mutant brood were dead, and the family home was engulfed in flames.

Now they had to deal with the pigman. Janie was sure Szat could make bacon out of him. He may have been only a runt, but so far, he'd caused some pretty impressive destruction. "Sweet ride," Szat said, sitting in the baggage compartment at the back.

"Thanks, it's the Spaz5000, the best..." John was interrupted by a roar from the bowels of the house. The walls shook as if caught in an earthquake.

"I think you better put your foot down," Szat said. "Or whatever it is crippled people do." John pressed the accelerator switch, and the wheelchair whirled down the long driveway to the gate. The crashing and banging in the house grew louder. Szat craned his head back and stared. "I don't like the sound of that."

"Me either." John sped up.

"Sounds like we might have upset Duke Sogash," Szat said. The front of the house exploded in shards of wood and glass. A ginormous hog the size of a Japanese hatchback, his pale skin smoking and on fire, landed on the porch and skidded through the railings. He clambered back onto his hooves and galloped toward them. "Sogash," squealed Szat.

John floored it. The gate at the end of the driveway was closed. There was no time to open it. Szat sent a flurry of fireballs shooting through the air and blew a section of the rotting fence apart. The Spaz5000 drove over the flaming planks, hurdled a ditch, and skidded onto the dirt road. A heavy downpour suddenly erupted. The wind violently rocked the trees. If Sogash could really control the weather, the forecast showed he was pretty pissed off.

"Which way?" John was freaking out and wide-eyed. Szat was trembling.

"The bus is to the right, but the main highway is that way," Janie said, pointing left. They sped down the road with Sogash in pursuit. The pig god's flesh smouldered. Drool hung from his gaping maw. Slowly he gained on them.

"This thing go any faster?" Szat said.

"No, this is its top speed."

"Dump the girl, she's slowing us down." Szat flung a fireball over his head. It went wide, sailed into the trees, and burst into the trunk of a ghost gum in a shower of sparks. Several birds, wings aflame, squawked and flapped over their heads.

"Sorry," John said and pushed Janie from the wheelchair. She landed hard on her ass.

"That's it, bros before hoes," Szat said. "Now let's get the fuck out of here."

"Fuck you, John." Janie couldn't believe John had done this to her. He'd condemned her to death. John skidded the wheelchair into a one-eighty-degree turn. As he sped past her toward Sogash with his giant, bent boner sticking out in front of him, he winked at her and grinned. "No, John, no, don't do it," Janie cried.

"What the fuck are you doing, you spastic?" Szat said.

"Going to Valhalla," John roared. He pulled the front wheels of the wheelchair into a wheelie. John gave Szat some garbled instructions. The demon's whole body began to grow and glow.

"I can't believe I've been summoned just for this shit," Szat moaned. Sogash's head was down and steam wafted from his nostrils.

The Spaz5000 and Duke Sogash slammed into each other. John, Szat and the pig god exploded as one giant ball of brilliantly bright light. A mushroom cloud shot upward into the air. A torrent of blood and gore rained down on Janie. Her ears popped from the deafening sound, and her eyes smarted from the blinding flash. A lump of misery was stuck in her throat as the light dwindled to a ghostly fog of acrid smoke. John couldn't have survived. She sniffed. The air was thick with the smell of burnt bacon.

SUMO SUPERSTAR

The remains of John's crispy cock slapped down onto the ground beside Janie and thrashed around in its death throes. Smoke billowed from both ends. Janie scrambled back, but not before the burnt appendage had sprayed the front of her top with dark blood.

She gazed down at the blackened, twitching phallus, the cause of so much of John's bitterness and harassment. The blast had rendered him into a jigsaw puzzle of human meat. Charred bits of the boy dangled from tree branches and peppered the dirt road. When Janie had first met John, only a few hours earlier, she'd thought he was a foul-mouthed, misogynistic twat with a giant stiffy, but after getting to know him during their time of peril, she'd realised he was a selfless and caring young man. He'd sacrificed his life for her, a girl who was little more than a stranger to him. John had gone to Valhalla on his Spaz5000 as a hero. She wept silently in gratitude for what he, Matt, and Garrett had done.

Janie wondered if Renée was still alive. Had she perhaps heard the explosion? Had she somehow managed to survive the woods and the monsters that lurked there? If the poor girl had been killed like John, Matt, Donna, and Garrett, Janie was now the lone survivor of this camping trip from hell. The awful thought rose up from deep within her stomach. Bile squirted out of her mouth and nose and frothed over her shoes. The tears continued to flow as the anguish spewed forth from her spasming gut.

Janie dragged herself to her feet and used the clean edge of her top to wipe her eyes and lips. Maybe Renée would be waiting at the bus. If the girl was alive, Janie couldn't leave her alone out here to face the pigman. She had to check. As she shuffled along the road, she tried to avoid looking at the smoldering body parts around her. Walking was hard going. Her fever grew worse. She was weak and dizzy, and every muddy step was a test of her endurance. The sun slowly rose above the trees, turning the dawn a fiery orange. Janie hobbled around yet another bend and came to a halt. The rear of the bus was visible at the edge of the road. The front of the vehicle was submerged in a swampy ditch of rainwater and broken reeds. Through a smashed window, the interior light flickered erratically as if it were fighting to stay alive.

Further ahead past the bus, revealed in the early morning light, a wooden bridge spanned the breadth of the river. Janie squinted. As she drew closer, she saw a hulking figure standing motionless on the middle of the platform. A sledgehammer was slung over its shoulder. The contours of a porcine head jarred with the rest of the human body. The shape grunted, snarled, and snorted. It heaved as if a roiling anger were trying to burst out of its muscular chest.

Janie stopped, unsure what to do. She could go back the way she'd come or run off into the woods, but the brute knew this place much better than she did. It would hunt her relentlessly until she was caught. Then it'd be the mincer for sure, or worse. Janie knew she was in no condition to outrun the pigman any longer. It was time to make a stand. She positioned herself near the railing. Savage River's waters raged below.

All her life she'd trained for this moment. Janie spread her legs so her feet were wide apart and placed her hands on her knees. While she kept one foot anchored, she lifted her other leg high in the air and drove it down onto the wooden planks with tremendous force, making the bridge shudder. An impressive feat for someone weighing less than one hundred pounds. She repeated the same exaggerated stomp with the other foot. Her parents' voices echoed in her ears as she stared down the pigman who edged toward her: *You know why we have to do this, my little Jonokuchi. We just want you to get better. Now, be a good girl and eat some more chankonabe.*

She'd been a lot heavier the last time she'd been in the sumo ring. Janie had spent six years in the prestigious Musaswashi sumo stable in Japan. The only westerner ever permitted. Training was eight hours a day, seven days a week. The rest of the time was spent cramming her face with Japanese stew, endless bowls of white rice, and drinking copious amounts of beer. She grew to love eating as much as the training regime to make her into a sumo superstar. Janie's weight ballooned. By sixteen years of age, she'd topped the scales at three hundred pounds. She was one of the heaviest girls in the dojo, and the most skilled. She'd won fourteen under eighteen sumo tournaments in a row. A Yokozuna, if ever there was one. Her father was so proud. Janie was living her father's sumo dreams for him.

One day everything changed. The family had to return to Australia when her mother's father was on his deathbed. The old man took so long to die she attended a local high school while they waited for him to pass on. At Ashburn High, she wasn't honoured as she was in Japan; instead, she was teased relentlessly for being so fat. Janie soon refused to eat. In desperation, her parents forced food into her, but she would go to the bathroom and make herself vomit. Her weight plummeted.

By the time her parents returned to Japan, she was only two hundred pounds, a weakling by sumo standards. Janie refused to go back to the stable to train and went on a hunger strike instead. Her father was distraught. His dreams had suddenly been dashed by his daughter's obstinacy. As Janie's sumo career slipped through their fingers, her parents returned to Australia where Janie spent the next two years of her life in and out of hospital psych wards.

The pigman scuffed the ground with his boots. Janie stomped her feet and grinned. The first rule of sumo was never to show any fear in front of your opponent. Besides, she'd taken down girls the size of the pigman before. Of course, she was heavier then. Bellowing, the pigman launched his great bulk forward and charged. He came on fast for his size, but Janie remained rigid. At the last moment she sidestepped, a perfect okuridashi. The pigman crashed through the railing at full force, but as he tumbled toward the water, he flung his arm back, grabbed Janie's ankle, and pulled her over the side with him.

They plunged into the churning river fifty feet below. The frigid water engulfed them, and the strong current swept them downstream. The pigman lost his grip. He fought against the undertow to close the gap, but he was a poor swimmer and could only doggy paddle. Janie kicked and stretched out her arms, but she was too exhausted to swim more than a few strokes. The current dragged her down to the riverbed. Water roared in her ears, and her lungs burned. Thick, grey silt clogged her mouth. Her clothing weighed heavily on her skinny frame. Cramps clutched her leg muscles, and the pain flashed through her body as if bolts of lightning shot up from the deep.

Splinters of morning sunlight pierced the water. She glimpsed Matt's ice blue eyes in its reflection. That bastard pigman was not going to win. Fuck him. Fuck his mama, his sister, and her butt-ugly, mutant kids. Fuck Sogash the pig god, and fuck this place. Janie fought her way to the surface and spat the mud from her mouth. She breathed deeply and concentrated on staying afloat, her legs pointing downstream. The pigman let out a tumult of high-pitched squeals, but showed no signs of tiring and was only a few feet away. The river rumbled. Bubbling water spurted into the air. A waterfall was ahead. Janie thrashed toward a rock jutting out of the water. She snatched at its surface slick with moss, but her fingernails scratched down the spongy coating without gaining purchase.

A smaller rock loomed into view. With her feet braced against it, she was able to grip onto its ridged surface. The pressure of the flowing river pounded against her. She was hauling herself up when the pigman grabbed her foot and pulled her to him. His hands closed around her neck and squeezed. She could smell his fetid breath. Hot gusts of air spurted from his nostrils. Teeth chattered and clacked inches from her face. Janie stared intently into the black, dull pupils; the eyes of a cruel and barbaric killer indifferent to the suffering of others, a being far more inhuman than the monsters of myths.

Janie's pulse pounded behind her own eyes. Her head was going to pop. Her vision blurring, they plummeted over the precipice and into the abyss. Together, they fell down a series of cascades, the seething water tossing and turning them around as if they were weightless. Their bodies were flung onto a cluster of sharp and jagged rocks. Janie braced herself, expecting to feel her bones shatter at any moment. Instead, the pigman cushioned her fall. The back of his head caved in on impact, and his brain splattered over the wet boulders. His hands dropped from her throat. Blood bubbled over his lolling tongue, and his eyes bulged, lifeless.

Janie slid back into the icy water and continued to drift downstream, too weak to swim to the bank. The river swirled under a low-lying branch. She reached up. Her fingers grazed the bark, but the current pulled her on. Ahead, a pile of debris from the river was clustered around a mass of twigs and foliage. Janie was being swept toward it. She grabbed at a stout piece of wood. It held, and she dragged herself to the bank. She lay there in a patch of sunshine, breathing in the swampy smell. Her throat was raw, and her side stung, but the woods were not safe.

She staggered through the trees and kept the sun to her right. Branches scratched and tore at her skin, but she was so numb and exhausted she didn't feel anything. Even though she was wet from the cold water, her body was burning up. She stumbled onto another dirt road. Not knowing which way to turn, she chose the easier path and walked down the hill. The unmarked road appeared endless; the trees soon closed in, and branches snapped and squeaked around her. Forms flitted and dashed overhead and between the tree trunks. She tried to hurry, but her body was shutting down. Her pace slowed to a shuffle.

Janie was startled from her fever dream by the blare of a horn. She turned around. Behind her, a car had stopped. A man and woman climbed out. The man appeared bemused, but the woman rushed over to assist the shivering, blood- and mud-covered girl. "Are you alright, sweetie? What happened? Do you need some help?" the woman asked.

She stroked the bedraggled hair from Janie's face. Janie sagged to her knees, but the woman helped her up and escorted her over to the car. The man, realising something was seriously wrong, quickly opened the door and helped usher the delirious girl onto the back seat. Two small children, a boy and a girl, stared curiously at the unexpected passenger slumped next to them. "Eww, she smells, Mummy," the little boy whined.

"And she's all soggy," the girl added. "I don't like her."

"P-p-please drive," Janie croaked. "They're out there." Her eyes darted along the tree line.

"Who's out there, sweetie?" The woman turned and stared at the woods.

"Come on, Gloria, let's get out of here," the man said. "We'll take her to the nearest police station. They can deal with… Oh, fuck!"

Dozens of naked figures sprinted from the trees, wielding stick spears and stone axes. "Fucking drive," Janie screamed.

The woman dived into the passenger seat. The man, his face white with shock, froze. His hands were taut around the steering wheel, and he stared in horror at the deformed pig child snarling at him from the other side of the windscreen. More feral pig children clambered over the car. They stabbed at the windows with their spears. The girl and boy burst out crying as one jumped onto the roof. "Drive," the woman screeched into the man's ear. She slapped him across the head.

Glass from the driver's side window exploded. A pig child, with purple tumours pulsating on its forehead, lunged through the jagged opening, but the man shoved him back. The mutant swung his crude axe into the man's neck. His hands snapped away from the steering wheel and clutched at the severed carotid artery spurting blood over the interior of the car and in the faces of his wife and kids. Panicked, he floored the gas pedal, and the car jolted forward. The vehicle weaved over the road. The children and the mother screamed hysterically. A pig child fell off the roof and was crunched beneath the tyres.

The man drooped over the steering wheel. Red bubbles frothed from his gaping neck wound. Janie could do nothing to save him. She crawled into the front and squeezed on top of the dying man to take the wheel. "Oh my god, oh my god, why are they doing this to us?" the woman wailed.

Janie looked in the rear-view mirror. Nude, snorting pig children dashed toward the crawling vehicle. Whipped up into a frenzy, they brandished their weapons and flung rocks. She stomped as hard as she could on the man's foot. The car sped down the dirt road, and the sound of squealing pigs was soon replaced by the sobs of young children and their distraught mother.

Made in the USA
Las Vegas, NV
17 October 2022

57546638R00080